Dempsey

THE B

Also available from Futura

DEMPSEY AND MAKEPEACE 1: Make Peace, Not War
DEMPSEY AND MAKEPEACE 2: Blind Eye
DEMPSEY AND MAKEPEACE 3: Lucky Streak
DEMPSEY AND MAKEPEACE 5: The Jericho Scam
DEMPSEY AND MAKEPEACE 6: Love You to Death

JOHN RAYMOND

Dempsey and Makepeace

THE BOGEYMAN

Based on an original screenplay
by Ranald Graham

Futura

A Futura Book

Series created by Golden Eagle Films

First published in Great Britain in 1986 by
Futura Publications, A Division of
Macdonald & Co (Publishers) Ltd
London & Sydney

ISBN 0 7088 3155 9

Typeset by Leaper & Gard Ltd, Bristol, England
Printed and bound in Great Britain by
William Collins, Glasgow

Futura Publications
A Division of
Macdonald & Co (Publishers) Ltd
Greater London House
Hampstead Road
London NW1 7QX
A BPCC plc Company

Chapter ONE

The killer waited patiently, oblivious to the cold or the uncomfortable surface of the roof. Beside him lay a high-powered rifle with telescopic sights. A pair of binoculars, mounted on a small tripod, were positioned on the parapet of the roof in front of him. Through them he got a perfect view of the cluster of portakabins in the middle of the desolate contruction site.

He looked at his watch. It wouldn't be long now. His target would soon be arriving. One squeeze of the trigger would climax weeks of careful planning . . .

A blue Mercedes van sped along the East India Dock Road in East London. Externally there was nothing to distinguish it from the other early morning traffic but it was carrying five armed men and one woman who was armed with both a .32 Smith & Wesson revolver and a video camera. They were all members of the special police unit known as S.I.10.

James Dempsey, who was in charge of the operation, leaned forward and said tersely, 'Now let me remind you that the point of this exercise is to catch these babies in the act. Not *before* so that Miller can get his fancy attorney to dance 'em outta court like last time — and not *after* — when somebody's already hurt. Got it?'

The other S.I.10 men murmured their assent. Makepeace remained silent, wondering why Dempsey was so unusually tense. She had never seen him this wound-up before. What was wrong?

'That's why the Sergeant is going to be recording the whole thing,' continued Dempsey, indicating the video camera she was holding on her lap. 'For evidence. So you cover her — and you cover her good or . . .' He didn't finish.

Makepeace said quietly, 'I don't need any nurse-maids, Dempsey. I know exactly what to do.'

'Yeah. You follow *my* orders, that's what you do. And if I say you get covered you get covered.'

Makepeace bit her lip. Was *this* the problem? Was Demspey being over-anxious on her behalf? If so he was being ridiculous. . .

'You think Miller and his mob are going to be well-tooled up, Lieutenant?' asked one of the S.I.10 men. His name was Phil Palmer and he was new to the unit. He couldn't keep a note of uneasiness out of his voice.

Dempsey glanced at the younger man. 'Yeah, sure to be. So remember what we worked out at the briefing. And hit 'em hard. Real hard. But never mind about Miller — he's mine. Understand?'

The men nodded.

'And you, Makepeace,' he added, glaring at her. 'You play it safe. No fancy stuff. You get a bullet hole in that beautiful hide of yours and I'll never talk to you again.'

She curled her upper lip, 'Could I have that in writing, Lieutenant?' she said coldly.

The killer watched as a cement truck moved across the construction site towards the group of cabins. The first of the performers had arrived, he told himself with bleak amusement. But he was only interested in the star of the show.

The cement truck pulled up about twenty yards from the portakabins. A burly man jumped down from the truck's cab. He was in his late forties with a face that would be much improved by a stocking mask. He was Charlie Miller and no stranger to stocking masks.

Clutching a sheaf of invoices in one of his massive hands he walked towards one of the cabins, whistling as he went. His two men waiting in the cement truck watched him with expressionless faces.

Miller knocked on the cabin door and pushed it open. An attractive young girl sitting at a desk looked up as he entered. Through an open office door he saw a middle-aged man operating a calculator.

'Er, I'm looking for Mr Johnson,' said Miller.

The girl shook her head. 'Not here,' she told him.

'Oh, er, I've got a load of concrete for him . . .'

'This is accounts,' said the girl, a touch impatiently.

'Oh, is it?' he said and gave her what he thought resembled an apologetic smile. In the distance he heard the sound of an approaching vehicle. He glanced back through the open cabin door and saw an armoured security van bouncing over the rough ground towards the cabin. He turned back to the girl. 'So where can I find Mr Johnson?'

'I've never heard of him,' she said. 'Maybe you've come to the wrong site.'

He heard the security van brake to a stop outside. He said to the girl, 'Yeah, maybe I have. Sorry to have troubled you ...' He turned and left. Outside he watched as two security guards got out of the van and went round to its rear. A door opened and another guard, inside the van, began to hand out sacks to them.

Miller looked at his watch. Right on cue he heard the sound of another approaching vehicle. It was a Jaguar, racing right towards the van. Miller immediately pulled a Luger from his jacket pocket.

'Don't move!' he yelled at the security men. 'Stand still or someone'll get shot!'

Simultaneously his two men leapt out of the cement truck brandishing pickaxe handles. As the two security guards stood there with shocked expressions on their faces Miller's men rushed up to them and knocked them sprawling onto the ground. Then they dragged the third guard out of the van and flung him face down on the ground as well.

'Get the bags!' ordered Miller. At that moment the Jaguar slewed to a halt beside the van. A heavily-built young man jumped out, ran to the rear and flung open the boot. While Miller kept the prone guards covered his two men started tossing the money sacks to the third man who threw them into the boot.

It was then that Miller heard the sound of a *third* approaching vehicle. 'Oh hell ...' he muttered. He turned to see a blue Mercedes van speeding across the site with the obvious intention of cutting off their get-away route. Before Miller had time to even react the van had screeched to a halt in front of the Jaguar and the

S.I.10 team were piling out . . .

On the distant roof the killer felt a mild jab of excitement. The rifle was mounted on the tripod now and he was surveying the scene through its telescopic sights. *Any moment now*, he told himself . . .

'Police!' yelled Dempsey, pointing his Colt Cobra at Miller. 'Drop it, Miller! Drop it!' Behind, Makepeace was calmly panning with the video camera from Miller to his two men who were standing there with the money sacks in their hands. Miller glanced back and saw that his third man — a new recruit to his organization who went by the name of Nick Lymon — was crouching behind the Jaguar with a shotgun in his hands.

Miller dropped his Luger and smiled at Dempsey. 'Hello again, Dempsey. You never give up, do you?'

'Never, Miller. As they say over here, you're *nicked* . . .'

'Dempsey!' cried Makepeace. She had spotted Lymon through the camera.

Lymon rose up from behind the Jaguar. The shotgun boomed. But Dempsey, alerted by Makepeace's warning, had already flung himself to the ground. The swarm of shotgun pellets passed overhead and punched holes in the side of the S.I.10 van.

Palmer and another of the S.I.10 men opened fire with their revolvers at Lymon but he'd ducked down behind the Jaguar. Swiftly he reloaded the double-barrelled shotgun . . .

On the warehouse roof at the edge of the construcion site the killer had Dempsey dead centre in his sights. The cross-hairs centred on Dempsey's head . . .

Lymon had thought fast. He knew he had no chance of winning a shoot-out so instead of firing back at the S.I.10 men he instead took aim at a stack of nearby fuel drums. He pulled the trigger . . .

Elsewhere another finger started to squeeze on another trigger . . .

The fuel drums blew up with a force that shook the ground. A ball of fire rose upwards and several of the fuel drums were sent spinning high into the sky, trailing smoke and fire as they went.

The blast was the one thing the killer hadn't counted on. Startled, he jerked the rifle as he fired. The bullet ploughed into the ground less than a yard from Dempsey's head. He didn't even notice.

The killer took aim for a second attempt but he was too late. Dempsey had leapt to his feet and was moving fast. The killer fired again but wasn't too surprised that he missed. This time the bullet hit the S.I.10 van. Then a cloud of thick smoke rolled across the scene, obscuring everything. The killer muttered one word under his breath.

It was chaos. Fuel drums were still exploding and the smoke was spreading fast. Dempsey got a brief glimpse of his quarry. He was making for the cement truck. Dempsey stopped and raised his Colt Cobra, waiting for another break in the smoke. It came. He took aim . . .

Someone charged into him, almost knocking him down. It was Miller. He tried to wrest the gun out of Dempsey's hand. Dempsey sank a hard left into Miller's ample abdomen. Miller made a whooshing noise as both air and fight left him simultaneously. Dempsey shoved him backwards then turned to take aim again. But his view was completely blocked by black smoke.

Then he heard the sound of the cement truck's motor roar into life. He fired blindly into the smoke, towards the source of the sound. The heavy vehicle was moving now. He could hear it coming straight towards him. He glanced back and realized if the truck didn't change direction it would crash into the cabin housing the site's accounts department.

He ran, shouting, towards the cabin. 'Everybody out! Run for it!'

A young girl stood frozen in the doorway, her eyes wide with shock. He pulled her roughly out. 'Move, damn you!' he yelled, giving her a push. She stumbled off into the smoke. A middle-aged man followed her out, then came a younger man and another girl.

'Anyone else in there?' Dempsey asked the latter as she ran past him. The girl said no. Dempsey turned. The cement truck emerged out of the smoke like some prehistoric monster. Dempsey had time for one shot. He saw the windshield shatter but the truck kept coming. He dived out of its path. The truck roared by him and hit the cabin. The lightly-built structure disintegrated under the impact and the truck didn't even slow down . . .

Dempsey fired again but heard his bullet clang harmlessly off its cement mixer. Then he lost sight of the truck in the smoke. 'Damn it!' he cried.

Somewhere in all the smoke he heard a car engine start up. It was the Jaguar. 'Miller . . .' groaned Dempsey. Cursing to himself he ran blindly through the smoke. The next thing he knew he'd collided with someone . . .

'Ow!' cried Makepeace as she landed hard on her bottom. She was still clutching the video camera.

Dempsey stared down at her with exasperation. The sound of the Jaguar's motor receded into the distance. 'You idiot!' he told Makepeace. 'Thanks to you Miller is getting away!'

Makepeace's face was covered with sooty grime. She wiped some of it off with the back of her hand and flashed her blue eyes angrily at Dempsey. 'No, he isn't . . . and please don't bother to help me up.'

He took her hand and hauled her roughly to her feet. 'If it's not Miller in that car then who is it?' he demanded.

'I don't know but it's *not* Miller. I just tripped over him back there.' She lifted her skirt. Dempsey saw that both of her knees were badly skinned. I'm going to be just one mass of bruises tomorrow . . .'

You left Miller by himself back there?!' exclaimed Dempsey. 'Why you crazy . . . .'

'Take it easy, Dempsey. He's not going anywhere. He's dead. Very, *very* dead.'

The killer dismantled his rifle and then packed the parts into a black leather case, along with the tripod and binoculars. His movements were calm and unhurried. There was no need to rush. No one knew he was there. Besides, he had a lot to think about. He had already damped down his anger over his failure to kill Dempsey. Self-recrimination was a waste of emotional energy. It also hindered the logical thought processes. He prided himself in being a very logical man. And anyway it hadn't been his fault. Who could have foreseen that explosion? He even felt a slight degree of professional admiration for the young crook who had set it off and used it to cover his escape. Fast thinking indeed.

But now he had to set up another plan to eliminate Dempsey or he wouldn't be able to collect the second half of the very substantial contract fee waiting for him back in New York. The problem was that his employers didn't want it known that Dempsey was the victim of a professional hit. They were most adamant on that point. It seemed that Dempsey still had friends as well as enemies in New York so it had to look as if Dempsey's death was a result of one of his London police operations that had gone wrong.

This morning's set-up would have been perfect. Okay, so they would have dug a rifle bullet out of Demspey and wondered where it had come from, but the only logical conclusion they could arrive at was that Miller had had an extra man hidden somewhere, armed with a rifle, as a back-up.

The killer sighed and took a final look at the smoke-strewn construction site. He'd come so close — and it might be weeks before he had another opportunity as good as this one had been.

But no matter. He'd do the job no matter how long it took.

He was a very patient man.

Chapter TWO

Spikings glared balefully across his desk at Dempsey and Makepeace. 'What a cock-up,' he growled. 'What a complete and utter cock-up.'

'Not completely,' protested Demspey. 'I mean, we got Miller, didn't we?'

'No — *we* didn't get Miller. Miller was got by one of his own men who happened to run over him with a cement truck!' yelled Spikings. 'If it hadn't been for that small piece of good fortune there's no telling where Miller would be by now. He certainly wouldn't have been grabbed by you or your team. All you managed to grab was *one* man . . .'

'It was all pretty confused, sir,' said Makepeace. 'There was a lot of smoke . . .'

'Yeah, and you let some young, green little hood blow smoke rings around all of you,' said Spikings sarcastically.

'He wasn't green,' muttered Dempsey. 'He was a pro. And I'm gonna get him.'

'Yeah, *sure* you are. You don't even know who he is!

'We will soon. we're having the shots of him on Makepeace's video film blown up right now.'

'What about the other one who got away? In the Jag.'

'Him we do have a name for,' said Makepeace. 'Brian Perry. Usually works as a wheelman. Lives in Harlesden. Local uniformed boys called round at his house. His wife said he's in Spain . . .'

'She would,' grunted Dempsey. 'Must have been his ghost driving that Jag.'

'They found the Jag yet?' asked Spikings.

'Yeah. In a side street in Greenwich. Wiped clean, of course. So was the cement truck. That ended up in Wapping.'

Spikings grimaced. 'Go on, get moving. I want some results — and *fast*.'

'So do I,' muttered Dempsey.

As they headed down the corridor towards their office they were intercepted by Chas, Spikings' harassed deputy. 'Here are your blow-ups,' he said, 'And your copy of the video tape as well.' He handed Dempsey several 10×8 photographs and the video cassette.

'Any luck identifying the guy?' Dempsey asked him.

'We've been through the computer files once already — nothing even close.'

'Yeah, well you gotta have something on him,' said Dempsey. 'This ain't no nobody. Young as he is he's got to have a track record somewhere.'

In the office Dempsey spread out the blow-ups across his desk. They were a little fuzzy but provided a good likeness of the young thug. Dempsey studied them closely, taking in the black, curly hair, the broken nose, the thin lips and the coldly arrogant eyes. He wasn't going to forget this face.

'You want to look at the tape again?' Makepeace asked him.

He sighed. 'Yeah. Might as well.'

He followed her over to the TV set in the corner of the office. Makepeace slipped the tape into the video machine and set it rolling. For the fifth time that afternoon they watched the morning's events being replayed on the screen.

'You could have held the damn camera steadier,' growled Dempsey.

'I trained as a police officer, not a Hollywood cameraman,' Makepeace told him stiffly. 'And the next time anything like this comes up *you* can be the one who . . .'

'Shush!' cried Dempsey. The young thug appeared on the screen. It was the moment when Makepeace had caught him sneaking round from the back of the Jaguar. Dempsey leaned forward, his expression intense. Makepeace glanced curiously at him. She had never seen him this tensed-up before.

'Bastard,' hissed Dempsey through clenched teeth as the shotgun went off just after the screen Dempsey had dived to the ground. He repeated the word a little later when the thug fired at the fuel drums. After that there wasn't much else to see except smoke. Dempsey kicked a filing cabinet out of frustration.

Makepeace looked at him and said, 'Dempsey, what *is* the matter with you? You've been behaving oddly all day.'

'Nothing's the matter with me,' he grunted, avoiding her eyes.

'Oh, don't give me that. There *is* something wrong. I know you well enough by now to tell when you're not your usual self. What's the problem?'

Dempsey suddenly sighed, ran his fingers through his hair, then sat down. 'Yeah, you're right. Something *is* bugging me but I don't know what. It's hard to explain, princess . . .'

'Try.'

'Well, for the last couple of weeks I keep getting this weird feeling — the "someone is walking over my grave" kind of thing. And also I feel like I'm being watched . . .'

Makepeace frowned. She didn't know what to say.

'I keep checking to see if I *am* being tailed by someone but there's never anyone there. So I guess it means I'm losing my grip. Getting paranoid, having anxiety attacks and all that.'

'That's ridiculous, Dempsey. You're not losing your grip,' she told him firmly.

'Oh yeah? Then how come I nearly got my head blown off by a goddamn kid this morning? If you hadn't warned me I'd be full of formaldehyde by now.'

'Oh Dempsey . . .'

'It's true! Spikings was right. The guy ran rings around me.'

'He ran rings round *all* of us. Look, maybe you're just rundown. Perhaps you need a holiday. You haven't stopped moving since you got here . . .'

He shook his head. 'No, it's not that. It's something else . . .'

At that moment Chas entered. He was looking more harassed than usual. 'I think we've got him.' He gave Dempsey a photograph. 'Mug-shot from a youth correction centre. Taken seven years ago . . .'

Dempsey stared at it. 'That's him alright!' he said excitedly. 'A lot younger, shorter hair and his nose isn't broken, but it's the same one. What's his name?'

'Nick Lymon. He was thirteen at the time.'

'What else have you got on him?'

'We're trying to dig it out now but there's some sort of problem.'

'What kind of problem?' demanded Dempsey loudly.

Chas flinched. 'I don't know yet. The computer is having difficulty in dredging anything else about Lymon out of the central system but I'm sure it's just a temporary glitch.'

'It better be,' growled Dempsey.

'Er, you said Lymon was armed with a shotgun, didn't you?' asked Chas hesitantly.

'Yeah. Why?'

'He wasn't carrying a rifle as well, was he?'

Dempsey glanced at Makepeace then turned back to Chas. 'He sure wasn't. Why do you ask?'

'Did you see *anyone* carrying a rifle at the site?'

Dempsey took a deep breath. 'No, I didn't. Now are you going to tell me why you're asking this or do I have to guess?'

Chas explained. 'When the forensic boys were checking over our van they found something else apart from shotgun pellets. They found a 9mm rifle bullet. It had gone through one side of the van and was lodged in the opposite side. The weapon that fired it was definitely a rifle. And a powerful one.'

Dempsey frowned and said, 'I sure as hell didn't see any rifle.'

'Neither did I,' said Makepeace.

Chas looked more worried. 'That means whoever fired it was some way off. I'll have the forensic boys take the van back to the site. If they park the van in exactly the same position it was in this morning they'll be able to align up the two holes and get a good idea where the shot came from.'

When Chas had gone there was a long silence in the office. Then Makepeace said, 'Miller was playing it tricky. Had a gunman covering the scene. We were lucky . . .'

'Yeah,' said Dempsey. He looked worried.

In the hired Ford Escort parked a block away from S.I.10 headquarters the killer frowned as he pushed the ear-piece more firmly into his ear.

Nick Lymon strode arrogantly down a side street off the Jamaica Road in Bermondsey. He was carrying a cloth bag over his shoulder. He stopped decisively at a blue Mini. Anyone who happened to be watching him would have presumed it was his car. They would have needed to be very close to see the large bunch of keys he was skilfully, and speedily, applying to the door lock. He hit the right one within 20 seconds. Once inside the car a second bunch of keys came into use. Another 20 seconds later and the Mini was moving off down the road . . .

The Mini pulled up outside a house in a small, leafy Surbiton street. Carrying the cloth bag Lymon went up to the front door and rang its bell. After a long wait it opened. Brian Perry peered suspiciously out. His eyes widened when he saw Lymon.

'Oh — hallo . . . you made it too, did you?'

Lymon pulled the shotgun out of the bag. Perry went white and backed into the hallway. Lymon followed and shut the door behind him.

'Hey, mate . . . what's your problem? There's no need for any rough stuff . . .' stuttered Perry.

Lymon silently gestured with the shotgun. Perry backed into the living room. He was sweating now. 'Look . . . Nick . . .'

Lymon glanced around the room then returned his attention to Perry. He raised his eyebrows.

'Er . . . um . . . the money, that's it, isn't it? Don't worry, it's right here, all of it . . .' Perry reached down behind a sofa and produced a black garbage bag. He tossed it towards Lymon. It landed at his feet. Lymon looked down at it and finally spoke.

'How much?'

'Six grand each.'

Lymon bent down and pulled one of the money sacks out of the bag. He gave a cursory glance inside it and nodded. Then he put two of the sacks in his cloth bag.

'Er, how did you know about this place?' Perry asked him worriedly.

'Miller. Told me he had this safe house for emergencies. What happened to him, anyway?'

Perry swallowed. 'Er, you mean you don't know?'

'Wouldn't be asking if I did, would I?'

'He's dead. I heard it on the radio. He got, er, run over. Seems you hit 'im with the, er, cement truck . . .'

Lymon shrugged. 'Tough.'

'Er . . . yeah . . . tough,' said Perry nervously. He'd realized by now that Lymon was a psychopath.

Lymon asked, 'Where did Miller get the job from?'

'He said Harry Rose.'

'Who?'

'Harry Rose. The promoter.' He gave a nervous laugh. 'You mean you never heard of Harry . . .?'

Lymon stepped closer to him. In a low, menacing voice he said, 'Are you laughing at me?'

Perry stared at the barrel of the shotgun. He started to tremble. 'No, no, mate . . . I wasn't, really . . .'

'I don't like being laughed at.'

''Course you don't, son. 'Course you don't.'

Lymon lowered the shotgun. 'I want this Harry's address. Now.'

'Sure, sure . . .' Perry hurriedly found a scrap of paper and a pen and scribbled down an address. He handed it warily to Lymon. Lymon pocketed it, then cocked the shotgun. Perry gave a gasp of fright and started to back away . . .

'No, son, no . . .' he breathed.

He kept on backing away until he was up against the wall. 'Please . . . don't . . .'

'You're gonna do something for me.'

'Anything! Anything!'

You're gonna forget you ever saw me. Right?'

Perry nodded vigorously. 'Right.'

''Cause if you do tell anyone about me I'm gonna catch up with you and blow your face off.'

Perry swallowed painfully and said in a hoarse voice, 'No worries, son. I've never seen you. *Ever.*'

'Good.' Lymon uncocked the shotgun, put it in the bag and silently left the room. When Perry heard the front door shut his body sagged against the wall. 'Bloody hell,' he sighed with relief.

Dempsey stared over Makepeace's shoulder at the

computer screen. 'That's it? That's all you got on this guy?'

'I'm afraid so.'

'But that's the same mug-shot as before. And the same basic info that was on his card. Just name, date of birth and nationality. Where's the rest of it? What about his school records? What about reform school — um, juvenile hall or whatever you call it here — there must be more than this!'

'Well, I've got some bad news for you, Dempsey. So try not to get too angry.'

'What bad news?' he asked suspiciously.

'The correction centre burnt down, and all the records with it, including Lymon's. This is all that survived. Arson was suspected but the guilty party was never apprehended.'

'Oh great!' Dempsey gave a snort of disgust. 'I can't believe what you're telling me — that that's all you got on this guy!? I mean, with all this computer equipment and you plugged into the brain centre of London at Scotland Yard!?'

'I knew you'd get angry,' said Makepeace quietly.

'Of *course* I'm angry! In this day and age you're telling me someone can go through life without leaving a trace on a computer somewhere!'

'Dempsey, you can't get information out of a computer if the information isn't there. There's no indication that Lymon has ever been arrested since leaving the centre, no indication that he's joined any of the armed services, applied for the dole or ever received medical treatment on the NHS. Nor has he ever opened a bank account or been given a credit card. I could go on.'

'I'm sure you could,' said Dempsey bitterly. 'You make it sound as if the guy doesn't even exist.'

'He's either very lucky or very clever.'

'Well, whatever he is I'm gonna get him. I'm gonna nail his ass if it kills me!'

'That's right — think positive,' said Makepeace drily.

Chas came into the office. 'We know where the gunman was this morning,' he said. 'On the roof of a warehouse way over on the opposite side of the site. He must be one hell of a shot . . .'

'Find anything on the roof?' asked Dempsey.

'No. The forensic boys checked it out thoroughly but got zilch. No discarded shells. No sign that anyone had been up there in years.'

'Sounds like a real professional,' said Makepeace. 'I'd certainly like to know who it was . . .'

'So would I,' growled Dempsey. He started to head for the door.

'Where are you going?' Makepeace asked him.

'To get some answers,' he growled over his shoulder.

Chapter THREE

Jim Pierce eyed Dempsey warily as he entered the cell. Pierce was a big man in his late thirties. Once he'd obviously been in good physical shape but now he was going to seed. Too much alcohol, guessed Dempsey. Nor did he look very bright.

'I wanna talk to you,' Dempsey told him.

'I've already told you and your mates all I've got to say,' said Pierce in a surly voice. 'So shove off.'

Dempsey gave him a hard stare. Then he said, 'Jim, ol' pal, you might as well play ball. Miller's dead and Perry's got away with the money. What have you got to lose?'

'I don't grass on me mates.'

'Lymon is a mate of yours?'

Pierce frowned. 'Who's Lymon?'

'Hey, don't play games with me, pal. I'm on a short fuse today. Lymon is the kid who almost took my head off with that shotgun this morning.'

I told you before — I'd never seen that geezer 'til today. I didn't know his name. Miller must have signed him up at the last moment.'

'How come I don't believe you?'

'It's the truth.'

'I suppose you'll say next that you didn't know anything about the guy with the rifle.'

'Guy with a rifle?' His eyes narrowed with suspicion. 'What are you trying to pull?'

'Miller had someone parked on a warehouse roof with a rifle. Our forensic guys have got proof. You wanna tell me all about it?'

Pierce shook his head. 'Nah, I don't believe it. Miller wouldn't do something like that. Not his style.'

'You saying you know nothing about it? You don't know who the guy is?' Dempsey asked.

'Nah. It's all news to me.'

'Looks like your boss didn't keep you very well informed. First Lymon and now this hidden gunman.'

Pierce shrugged. 'Seems so.'

'Well, pal, you'd better come up with *something* useful to tell me real quick or I'll see to it you're put away for a ten-year stretch at least. I'll fit you up so good and tight you'll think you're in a straight-jacket.'

Pierce went pale. 'Look, mate, I've got a wife and kids. I can't go inside for ten years . . . no way . . .'

'Then tell me where I can find Perry.'

'I told you — I don't grass . . .'

'Then get Perry to look after your wife and kids. He can afford to with all the money he's got now . . .' Dempsey turned. He was just opening the cell door when Pierce said, 'Wait, copper, wait!'

Dempsey turned back to him. 'Yeah?'

Pierce took a deep breath and said, 'Miller's got this safe house — in Surbiton. Perry's probably there.'

'The address,' said Dempsey coldly.

Nick Lymon parked the Volvo in Denmark Street — he'd already dumped the Mini — and got out. He checked the address again and stopped outside a seedy-looking theatrical agency. There were a number of fading posters in the window advertising musicals, pop concerts and boxing matches.

Still carrying his cloth bag Lymon pushed open the door and went inside.

A fat man in his late fifties sat behind a desk that was propped up on one corner by a pile of telephone books. The man, like his suit and his office, had seen better days. He scowled at Lymon. 'Who are you?' he demanded.

Lymon took the shotgun out of the bag, pointed it at the fat man, then calmly sat down facing him. 'Harry Rose?'

The fat man nodded, his eyes alternating between the gun and Lymon. 'Mind if I smoke?' he said finally.

'Go ahead. They're your lungs.'

Rose grabbed a pack of Marlboro from the top of the desk and, with difficulty, pulled out a cigarette. He had just as much difficulty lighting it. After taking a deep drag on it he seemed to become more self-controlled. He managed a weak smile at Lymon and said, 'Whatever you're auditioning for I don't think I got an opening, son.'

Lymon didn't smile back. 'You hear what happened to Miller this morning?'

'Yeah. Bad business. But what's it got to do with you?'

'A lot. I was in on the job. Nearly got caught.'

'You were working with Miller? For how long?'

'Not long.'

'Close thing was it this morning?'

'Very close.'

'You were lucky.'

'Yeah.' Lymon's voice gave nothing away. It was as flat as an ironing board.

Rose took another long drag on his cigarette and said, 'So what can I do for you, son?'

'You can stop calling me *son* for a start.'

'Oh, sure, sure — whatever you say, s—, er, mate.'

'Now I'll tell you what I want from you. I want some jobs. Like you gave Miller this morning. But better. Know what I mean?'

'The job was solid. Someone must have blabbed. One of Miller's boys. A pint too many in a pub. It's always the way. It's amazing what you can overhear in pubs sometimes. Idiots who don't think anyone's listening. They start bragging about a job and end up bragging themselves right behind bars. More villains have put themselves into prison than were ever caught by the filth. It's a fact.'

Lymon just stared at him silently.

'Look, it wasn't me, son — I mean, er, mate. You can trust me one hundred percent all the way.'

Lymon still said nothing.

'Ask anyone, anyone at all,' said Rose, a touch of desperation entering his voice. 'Harry Rose is as solid as they come.'

'You'd better be. Anything goes wrong with a job you give me and I'll make you swallow this shotgun. Both barrels. Get my drift?'

Rose nodded frantically.

Brian Perry had just entered the hallway with a sandwich in one hand and a glass of beer in the other when the front door suddenly exploded inwards. The next thing he knew a large, tall man was coming straight at him brandishing a revolver the size of a small cannon. Behind was a woman with blonde hair.

Perry yelped and dropped both sandwich and beer.

Dempsey grabbed him and flung him against the wall. 'Go on, spread 'em!'

Pierce, with his face pressed to the wall, managed to cry, 'I'm not armed!'

He was roughly searched then pulled round again. He recognized the pair of them now. They had been among the group of cops at the site that morning. 'How'd you find me?' he asked, a sick, sinking feeling in the pit of his stomach. He'd been nicked . . .

Dempsey holstered his gun and said. 'Where's Lymon?'

'Who?'

'Lymon. The kid with the shotgun.'

'Oh, him. I never seen him before.'

Dempsey groaned. 'Not you too.' He grabbed Perry by the shoulders and threw him down the hallway. Perry gave a cry of pain and fear as he went sprawling along the floor. Dempsey followed and hauled him to his feet. 'Now talk!'

Shaking, Perry gasped, 'My life! M. . .Miller brought him in as a last minute replacement! He was a total stranger!'

For a job like that? And with a shotgun? What did Miller do — go round to the nearest Youth Opportunities Scheme and ask for a kid with experience at armed robbery?'

'I didn't know nothing about shooters. I never carry one, and that's a fact!'

'Oh yeah?' sneered Dempsey. 'And you didn't know anything about the other guy either? The one on the roof? with the rifle?'

Perry looked blank. 'Wha . . .?'

Dempsey bounced him off the wall. 'Try again.'

'Honest, I don't know nothing about any rifle!'

Makepeace came out of the living room carrying two sacks. 'I found this.'

'Is it all there?' asked Dempsey.

'Nope.'

'How much is missing?'

'Six grand. Half of it.'

Dempsey turned back to Perry. 'Your turn.'

'That's all I got . . .'

'We can *see* that. So where's the rest of it?'

'I dunno . . . honest.'

Dempsey clenched his right fist and waved it under Perry's nose. We're not playing Trivial Pursuits here, pal. I want a serious answer or I give your dentist the challenge of his career.'

'Take it easy, Dempsey,' warned Makepeace.

'I'm tired of taking it easy. This guy talks now or he won't talk again until they take the wire out of his jaw.'

Perry swallowed noisily and said, 'Lymon took it.'

'When?'

'Over an hour ago. He came and took his cut. I thought he was gonna do me in and all! The guy's a psycho!'

'That's news? We know that. We want to know where we can find him.'

'I dunno. He didn't tell me nothing . . . arghhh!'

Dempsey bounced him off the wall again then

grabbed him by the throat.

Makepeace said worriedly, 'Dempsey, don't . . .'

Ignoring her, Dempsey said, 'Let's go back to the guy with the rifle again.'

His eyes bulging, Perry gasped, 'I . . . told . . . you . . . Don't know nothing 'bout a guy with a rifle . . . swear it . . .'

'Well, I'm not buying that, pal. You either tell me something about him or Lymon. Take your pick, I'm not fussy.' Dempsey increased the pressure on Perry's throat.

Perry started to choke. Makepeace stepped forward and started to pull on Dempsey's arm 'Let him go! You're killing him!'

Several long seconds ticked by before Dempsey sighed and relaxed his grip. Perry desperately sucked in air. 'All . . . I . . . know . . . know . . . about Lymon is he's a boxer . . .'

'What? He tell you that?'

Perry shook his head. 'Nah . . . it's written . . . all over him. Used to box myself. The way he moves . . . his nose . . . he's a boxer okay . . .'

Dempsey let him go. 'Christ, yes!' he exclaimed, making Perry start. 'Why the hell didn't I see that myself?!' Unexpectedly, he grinned widely and gave Perry an almost friendly pat on the shoulder. Perry shrank from his touch. 'Thanks, pal,' said Dempsey. He turned to Makepeace. 'Lymon's a boxer.'

Mystified, Makepeace said, 'Well, hip, hip hooray, but why is that a good thing?'

But Dempsey didn't answer her. Instead he said to Perry, 'You all right, pal?'

Perry nodded warily, his eyes still fixed fearfully on Dempsey.

Makepeace took Perry by the arm. 'Come on — let's

go.' As she led him out the front door she said, 'You've got to excuse Lieutenant Dempsey. He's not himself today.'

This information didn't seem to reassure Perry.

Neither Dempsey nor Makepeace paid any attention to the youth with the punk hair style who was tinkering with his motorbike on the footpath outside. After they had bundled Perry into their car and driven off, the youth watched them go then gave up the pretence of working on his machine. He put the spanner in one of the bike's two leather pouches, got on the bike, started its engine and sped off.

Some time later he entered a small, dingy drinking club in Denmark Street which was almost directly opposite Harry Rose's premises. Lymon was at the bar. The youth sidled up to him.

'Well?' said Lymon quietly.

'I could do with a drink, Nick.'

'Talk first.'

'The Old Bill come. Took him away.'

'Uniformed?'

'Nah. Plain clothes.'

'You sure they were cops?'

'Yeah. I heard them talking. They were cops okay. But one was a bird. Good looker too.'

Lymon frowned. 'A bird?'

'Yeah. Blonde. Nice legs . . .'

'What about the bloke?'

'A big geezer. A real hard case. Kicked the door in like it was balsa-wood. He was tooled up too. So was she. Funny thing was though, he was a Yank.'

'A Yank?' He remembered the big cop at the site that morning. With the American accent. And the policewoman with the camera had been blonde. 'Bastards . . .' he muttered.

'Ol' Perry looked in bad shape when they brought him out. Shaking like a leaf. Wouldn't count on him not to start talking . . .'

'He does and he's dead,' said Lymon, pushing a twenty pound note across the bar to the youth. 'That goes for anyone who grasses on me. *Anyone.*' He stared at the youth, who swallowed and nodded.

Spikings burst into the S.I.10's outer office where Chas sat transcribing a tape. 'Chas, I want to talk to you!'

But Chas, encased within his earphones, carried on working.

'Chas!' bellowed Spikings.

Chas gave a start and turned. Then he pulled off the earphones. 'Yes Chief?'

'I've just had a few words with this Perry character. What the hell did you do to him?'

'Nothing!' protested Chas, looking affronted.

'He was shaking so much his teeth were chattering. Looked on the verge of a nervous breakdown.'

'Well, that's the way Dempsey brought him in.'

Spikings frowned. 'He did, did he? Well, you'd better get Perry a doctor bloody quick, because between the two of them, Lymon and Dempsey have got him crawling up the wall.'

'Right, Chief.' Chas picked up a phone and started punching out a number.

'And speaking of our over-excitable resident Yank, where is he?'

'He said he and Makepeace were going off for a bite to eat while they waited for the pubs to open.'

'He said *what*!!!?' bellowed Spikings.

Chapter FOUR

As they entered the 'Thomas À Beckett' pub in Whitechapel, Makepeace said in a low, annoyed voice, 'For the last time, Dempsey, are you going to tell me what we're doing here or do I have to beat the information out of you.'

Dempsey pulled her to a halt and made a sweeping gesture at the interior of the pub. 'What do you see, princess?'

'A lot of men drinking. And apart from the barmaids I appear to be the only woman in the place. Charming.'

'I mean what do you see on the *walls*?' said Dempsey impatiently.

Makepeace looked and sighed. 'Loads of boring old boxing paraphernalia. Fight posters and faded photographs of half-naked men holding up their fists.' She wrinkled her nose. 'I can almost smell the stale sweat.'

'And what did Perry say about Lymon?'

'That he thought he was a boxer.' She nodded, 'Yes, I see that there is a connection but I still don't see the *point* of coming here. Do you expect Lymon to drop in for a drink or something?'

Dempsey scowled 'And you call yourself a policewoman. Come on . . .' He led the way through the crowds towards the bar. Not unexpectedly, Makepeace attracted a good deal of attention from the exclusively male clientele but there was one man, sitting alone at a table, who was more interested in Dempsey. The man was in his mid-thirties. He was pale-skinned, had blond hair that was cut very short, blue eyes that were so light-coloured they appeared almost grey and an aquiline nose. He was well built and dressed in blue jeans, blue shirt and black leather jacket. Inside the jacket, in a special pocket, nestled a 9mm Browning automatic complete with silencer.

'What do you want to drink?' Dempsey asked Makepeace.

'A glass of chilled champagne, please'.

The barmaid stared at her. Nearby a customer sniggered and dug his mate in the ribs with his elbow. Dempsey gave Makepeace a murderous look. 'Have a lager,' he told her. 'You're not in Claridges.'

'I said I want a glass of champagne, please,' said Makepeace firmly.

'We ain't got any,' said the barmaid.

'Give her a half of lager,' growled Dempsey.

'Have you any Pimms?' Makepeace asked the barmaid.

'You what?'

Makepeace sighed. 'I'll have the half of lager.'

Dempsey rolled his eyes. 'Jesus, you really know how to blend in with the background, don't you?'

'It depends on the background. Besides, *you* brought me here. You must have realized I would rather stand out in this Neanderthal's drinking hole.'

'Shush, not so loud,' cautioned Dempsey, glancing round worriedly.

'Don't worry,' said Makepeace coolly. 'I don't think anyone here knows what "Neanderthal" means.'

'Shut up and drink your lager,' growled Dempsey. 'I've got work to do.'

'This I must see . . .'

Dempsey gave her a final scowl and turned to the man leaning on the bar beside him. The man, in his early forties, had cauliflower ears and ridges of old scar tissue over both eyebrows. As far as Dempsey was concerned he looked very promising material.

'My name's Jim,' he said, offering his hand. 'How ya doin'?'

After a moment's hesitation, and a glance at Makepeace, the man shook Dempsey's hand. 'Mine's Terry.'

'Well Terry, you might be able to help me out. I'm looking for a young boxer. Name of Nick Lymon. Have you heard of him?'

Terry screwed up his face then shook his head. 'Nah. Can't say I have.'

Dempsey produced one of the blow-ups of Lymon from his pocket. 'This is the guy.'

Terry examined the photograph. Then he slowly nodded. 'Yeah. I've seen him around.'

'Do you know where I could find him?'

'Nah. But old Jim Kelly would know.'

'Jim Kelly?'

'Yeah. A trainer. I've seen that kid with him in here quite a few times.'

'And where can I find Jim Kelly?'

A crafty look appeared in Terry's eyes. 'Depends.'

'Depends on what?' Dempsey asked him.

'On how much you're willing to pay.'

'Would a tenner do the job?'

'I reckon so.'

Dempsey turned to Makepeace. 'Princess, give the guy ten quid.'

'Again? You owe me a hundred already,' she protested.

'Just can it and give him the money. This is important.'

'So's my overdraft,' said Makepeace, but she took her wallet out of her shoulder bag and produced two five pound notes. Dempsey grabbed them and handed them to Terry.

Terry said, 'Old Jim Kelly has a place down in the docks not far from here. In Northey Street. A warehouse with a big painted sign saying MINTER TEA on the front. He lives on the first floor.'

'Thanks,' said Dempsey, not noticing the man with short blond hair who had pushed his way to the bar behind Terry.

'What's this all about anyway?' asked Terry. 'Why are you looking for this kid?'

'I've seen him in action. I like his style. I want to make him an offer,' said Dempsey.

'Oh,' said Terry. 'In the fight game, are you?'

'In a manner of speaking, yeah,' nodded Dempsey.

Terry looked enquiringly at Makepeace. 'What about her? She in the boxing game as well?'

'The princess? Nah,' said Dempsey with a straight face. 'She's a lady mud wrestler. A champ, in fact. With any luck she'll net the world title next year.'

Terry looked at Makepeace with an expression of awe. 'Wow,' he said.

'Ha-bloody-ha,' muttered Makepeace as they left the pub.

'Hey, the guy was real impressed by that. I think he fancied you.'

'Every man in that bar fancied me.'

Dempsey shook his head. 'With an ego the size of the one you got it's a wonder you can fit it in your apartment.'

'*My* ego? You're a fine one to talk about egos! You're the most egotistical man I've ever met . . .!'

As they walked, bickering, to their car they didn't see the man with the cropped blond hair emerge from the pub behind them.

'What a dump,' said Dempsey, staring at the dilapidated front of the former tea warehouse.

'I bet it has rats,' said Makepeace uneasily. 'I hate rats.'

'Stay here then, 'he told her. 'I'll go talk to the Kelly guy by myself.'

'This is uncommonly gallant of you, Dempsey. Thanks.'

'My pleasure, princess,' said Dempsey as he got out. He crossed the street and climbed the rickety fire escape up to the first floor doorway. There was a light shining under the door. *Good,* he thought as he rapped hard on the dirt-stained wood.

After a long wait the door was finally prised ajar. An old man peered out through the gap. The damp remains of a roll-your-own cigarette drooped from the corner of his mouth. 'Yeah?' he said hoarsely. 'What you want?'

'Jim Kelly?'

'I might be. I might not be,' said the old man,

giving Dempsey a suspicious glare. 'What's it to you?'

'I want to talk to you, if you are Kelly.'

'Talk away.'

'Mind if I come in? It's kinda cold out here.'

After a pause the old man grudgingly opened the door all the way. Dempsey entered. He found himself in a large, musty, dimly lit room that was crammed with packing cases and assorted pieces of junk. There was a bed in one corner that looked as if its sheets hadn't been changed since the Romans left Britain. A nearby table was covered with unwashed plates, empty tins, Guinness bottles and food scraps.

'Nice place you've got here,' said Dempsey.

The old man made a snorting sound that could have meant anything. Then he said, 'What do you want to talk about?'

'I'm looking for someone. I heard you might know where he is.'

'Who told you that?'

'That doesn't matter. Don't you want to know who I'm looking for?' Dempsey was wandering around the room as he talked. He paused in front of a punch bag and gave it a tentative jab.

'So who are you looking for?' asked Kelly warily.

'Nick Lymon,' said Dempsey, turning to face him.

'Nicky, eh?' The old man rubbed the white stubble on his chin. It made a rasping sound. 'Why are you looking for him?'

'I want to talk to him.'

'Yeah?' The old man narrowed his eyes. 'You're from New York, aren't you?'

'That's right. I came all this way just to see you so don't disappoint me.'

'I been to New York once. Back in the 1950s. I was managing a young middle-weight name of Bernie

Wright . . .' The old man's voice took on a wistful tone. 'Thought he was a sure thing, that he'd go to the top for sure. But he got KO'd in his first fight at Madison Square Garden. He was never the same after that. Broke his spirit . . .'

'About Nick Lymon,' said Dempsey. 'How long have you known him?'

'Couple of years. Been training him. He's got a lot of potential.'

'Yeah, so I've heard,' said Dempsey drily. 'When was the last time you saw him?'

'About a month ago. Said he was going to visit an aunt in Birmingham.'

'Really?' said Dempsey who didn't believe a word of it. He walked over to the table and stared at the mess. Then he noticed a half-empty cup of coffee with a stubbed-out cigarette lying in the saucer. The cigarette had a filter tip. And Kelly was smoking a hand-rolled one.

Casually, Dempsey let his gaze wander around the room. 'Whereabouts does he live?' he asked. 'When he's in London, I mean.'

'Er, well, the last six months Nicky was stayin' here,' admitted Kelly.

'Yeah? That's interesting,' said Dempsey. He'd noticed a curtained alcove behind a stack of packing cases.

'You still haven't told me why you want to talk to Nicky,' said the old man.

Dempsey started to move towards the alcove. 'He owes a fine on an overdue library book.'

'Where you goin'?' cried Kelly when he saw Dempsey heading towards the alcove.

Dempsey didn't answer. He roughly pulled the stained curtain to one side. Nick Lymon stared at him with surprise.

'Hi Nicky,' said Dempsey. 'Fancy finding you here . . .'

Without warning Lymon sprung from the alcove and unleashed a brutal right at Dempsey's jaw. Caught off-guard Dempsey grunted with pain as Lymon's fist connected with his chin. He rocked back on his heels, stars exploding in his eyes. Lymon followed up with a left jab to Dempsey's heart. Dempsey heard a roaring sound and the next thing he knew he was on the floor.

Lymon raced off down between a row of packing cases. Dempsey shook his head in an effort to clear it then got to his feet. He saw Lymon climbing up a steep flight of wooden stairs. Dempsey gave chase. By the time he'd reached the base of the stairs Lymon had disappeared through the door at the top.

His ears still buzzing and his jaw throbbing Dempsey charged up the stairs. He threw open the door and found himself on a fire escape landing on the side of the warehouse. Overhead he heard the clatter of Lymon's shoes on the landing above.

Dempsey drew his Colt Cobra and started to climb the fire escape as fast as possible. As he emerged up onto the next landing the toe of a shoe caught him under the chin. Again stars exploded behind his eyes and he fell backwards, desperately scrabbling for a handhold to prevent himself from falling all the way down to the next landing. In his efforts to save himself he dropped the Colt . . .

The kid is playing me for a sucker all the way! he told himself angrily.

With mounting fury he climbed back to the second landing. Lymon had reached the top of the ladder by now and was going onto the roof.

By the time Dempsey arrived at the top Lymon was on the opposite side of the flat roof. As Dempsey watched, Lymon launched himself into the air then landed on the roof of the adjacent building.

When Dempsey arrived at the edge of the roof he hesitated. The gap between the buildings was about six feet. 'Oh hell,' he muttered. He backed up several yards then ran as fast as he could. Suddenly there was nothing beneath him but a three-storey drop. Then, to his relief, he was landing on the next roof . . .

But his ankle gave way beneath him and he fell full-length with a bone-jarring crash.

'This is definitely not my day,' he muttered as he dragged himself painfully upright again and continued to give chase.

By the time he reached the other side of the roof Lymon was halfway down another fire escape that led down to a narrow, dark alley. Dempsey, panting heavily by now, started after him.

When he got to the bottom he could see Lymon's retreating figure outlined at the far end of the alley. It was beginning to seem hopeless to Dempsey — Lymon had youth on his side — but he refused to give in . . .

He'd taken only a few strides when suddenly something stepped out of a recess in the alley wall. Dempsey only had time to register a black shape and a pair of disembodied eyes before he was hit in the side of the neck by what felt like a length of two-by-four. After that — nothing . . .

The killer massaged the edge of his right hand as he stood looking down on his victim with satisfaction. It had all worked perfectly. When Dempsey's dead body was discovered it would be presumed that Lymon had killed him in a hand-to-hand struggle.

Then, beneath his black ski mask, the killer frowned. He bent down for a closer look. Yes, there was no mistake — Dempsey was still breathing.

Damn it! thought the killer. Dempsey was even tougher than he looked.

He rolled Dempsey onto his back, exposing his throat. Then, bending over him, he raised his right hand to deliver the death blow . . .

Chapter
FIVE

'Freeze!'

The killer froze, but turned his head. Dempsey's partner, the blonde, stood there less than four yards away. Her arms were stretched out in front of her. In her hands was a .32 revolver pointing straight at him. It was very steady.

The killer was surprised. How had she managed to get this close without him hearing her? Either she was very good or he was being ridiculously careless.

'Move away from him and raise your hands!' she ordered crisply. He did as she said.

Makepeace was confused. Who *was* this strange figure dressed all in black? It certainly wasn't Lymon so why had he attacked Dempsey? 'Who are you?' she asked him.

He remained silent. His eyes regarded her with a disquieting calmness through the slits in the ski mask.

'I said, who are you?' she repeated. 'Come on, *say* something . . .!'

She glimpsed something glittering in his raised right hand. Her reflexes saved her. Before her conscious mind had even registered what was happening her body was twisting to one side. The knife swished past her, missing her by inches. Off balance, she fired blindly. The flash from the barrel momentarily dazzled her. Seconds later, when her vision cleared, she was amazed to see that there was no trace of the mystery figure. She had expected to find him stretched out before her. How had she missed at this close range? And how had he managed to vanish so quickly . . .? She shuddered.

Dempsey groaned.

'I still think you should see a doctor,' said Makepeace. 'That's a nasty bruise you have there. He might have fractured one of the vertebrae in your neck.'

'Nah,' said Dempsey sourly. 'I'll be okay.' He was sitting on a couch in the living room of Makepeace's Holland Park flat and applying a towel full of ice cubes to the side of his neck.

'You don't look okay. You look like Miller looked after he got run over by that cement truck.'

'I tell you I'm okay. A few hours shut-eye and I'll be fine again. But I could do with some more medicine . . .' He held out his empty glass. With a sigh she refilled it with the expensive fifteen-year-old malt whisky that had been a gift from her father. Then she winced as Dempsey took a couple of ice cubes from the towel and dropped them in the glass.

'What a thing to do to good whisky,' she said disapprovingly.

'It's not so hot,' he said after he'd taken a large swallow. 'Too bland. Lacks bite.'

'I'm sorry I'm all out of methylated spirits. I'll try and stock up on a few gallons before your next visit.'

'You're all heart,' he muttered and took another large swallow.

'Have you had any bright ideas yet on the identity of our mystery man?' she asked as she poured herself some of the whisky. No point in wasting it *all* on Dempsey.

Dempsey shook his head, then grimaced with pain. 'Nah, not a one. All I know is that I want to get my hands on him *fast*. I'm going to break his goddamn neck!'

'There was no one else in that room apart from Lymon and the old man?'

'Not that I saw.'

'So he had to be waiting around outside the whole time,' she said, frowning. 'But why? Has Lymon got his own minder or something?'

'You got me, princess.'

'And he was obviously *prepared*,' continued Makepeace thoughtfully. 'That black costume, the mask, the throwing knife. Yet how could he have known we were coming? Lymon was certainly taken by surprise when you showed up, wasn't he?'

'He sure was,' said Dempsey.

'And the *speed* at which he moved. The man is obviously a trained athlete. He's no common London villain. In fact, you know what he reminded me of — a Ninja.'

'A what?'

'You know, one of those Japanese assassins you see in the movies and on TV. Always dress in black, somersault over walls backwards and throw those star-shaped knives . . .'

'Why would a Ninja be after me? I haven't arrested any Japs.'

'I'm not saying he *is* one; I'm saying that's what he reminded me of. An assassin. He was definitely about to kill you when I arrived on the scene.'

Dempsey looked thoughtful. 'You think maybe it was the same guy who was on the roof with the rifle this morning?'

'It's a possibility,' admitted Makepeace. 'But that doesn't explain why he's trying to kill you now. Miller's dead.'

'Maybe that's why. Revenge. The guy might have been a close friend of Miller's. Or a relative.'

Makepeace shook her head. 'Our file on Miller and friends is pretty comprehensive. I can't think of anyone in it who could be the man in black. No, my theory is Miller hired a hit-man. To get *you*. After all, you'd been on Miller's back these past few months. He knew you'd nail him sooner or later so he brought in someone to knock you off first.'

Dempsey leaned back on the couch, still holding the wet towel to his neck. 'Yeah,' he said wearily. 'You could be right.'

'The more I think about it the more I know I'm right,' said Makepeace excitedly. 'Remember what you said this afternoon? Your feelings of being watched recently. Your feelings of paranoia? Well, you weren't imagining things! You *were* being followed!'

'Yeah,' he sighed.

'Well, don't you see?' she persisted. 'You weren't losing your grip after all.'

He regarded her wearily. 'Oh yeah? What about tonight. I get out-boxed by a punk kid who then shoots off leaving me floundering in his wake like an old garbage scow. Then I get chopped down by this other guy who I didn't even *see* . . .'

'You can't blame yourself, Dempsey. You were taken by surprise both times.'

'That's two times too many in this game. Nah, I got to face it, princess, I'm losin' my edge. I'm getting old . . .'

'Oh, *really*!' cried Makepeace, exasperated. 'Talk about a load of maudlin self-pity! I can't believe this is the same James Dempsey I used to know and detest! You sound like a *wimp*.'

Anger flared in Dempsey's eyes. 'I ain't no wimp,' he growled.

'Good. Now pull yourself together and stop acting like one. So you had a bad day. So what? Everyone has bad days. You were up against some tough opposition. Lymon is a ruthless thug, not to mention a trained boxer, while our Man in Black is obviously a professional killer. Yet you're still alive . . .'

'Thanks to you,' he muttered.

'Hey, don't make it sound as if I did you a bad turn by saving your life! What is it — you resent being saved by a mere woman?'

He held up a hand. 'Sorry, princess. You're right — that was out of line . . .'

She stared at him in wonder. 'Now I've heard everything. Dempsey apologizing to me! You really are in a bad way. Maybe it's time you got some sleep. You might be more your old self in the morning.'

He yawned. 'Yeah, you're right. Let's turn in.'

'I'll go fetch you some blankets and a pillow.' Makepeace got up and went outside. When she returned with the bedding Dempsey grinned at her. 'Look,' he said, 'Instead of going to all this trouble why don't I just join you in your bed? I'm sure it's big enough.'

She raised her eyebrows at him. 'Dempsey, while I'm prepared to go to serious lengths to help restore your faith in your masculinity, *that* is a sacrifice I'm not prepared to make.' She dumped the bedding on the couch beside him and marched off towards her bedroom door. At the door she paused and said to him, 'Besides, I promised my father I would never sleep with a social inferior.'

The door closed behind her, leaving Dempsey wondering if she was being serious or not. With her he could never tell. A short time later the door opened again. For a brief, happy, moment Dempsey thought she had changed her mind about his proposal but his hopes were torpedoed when she said, 'Oh, and help yourself to more whisky. I know you would have anyway but I just wanted to ease your conscience. 'Night.'

Dempsey stared at the closed door and muttered, 'Bitch.'

The killer parked his car in front of the small Earl's Court Hotel where he was staying and got out slowly. The wad of paper handkerchiefs that he had pressed against the wound in his chest under his leather jacket was already soaked with blood.

He winced with pain as he reached into the car and lifted out his bag. In the lobby he walked swiftly to the reception desk and asked the middle-aged woman behind it for his key. He was worried that he might start dripping blood on the floor. To his annoyance she persisted in a bout of cheerful small talk — asking him how he was enjoying his stay in London, what part of America he came from and so forth. It took an effort of will on his part to remain calm and polite. It was an important rule in his profession never to arouse curiosity by behaving unusually. He wanted people to forget him as soon as they saw him . . .

Finally she handed over his key and he was able to escape. Once inside his room he hurried into the bathroom and stripped off his jacket and shirt. Then he soaked a towel in cold water and washed the blood from his right side. He was relieved to see that it looked worse than it really was. Makepeace's bullet had cut a three-inch-long groove through his thick serratus anterior muscle but it wasn't very deep. It was bleeding badly but he felt certain that he could staunch the flow without having to have the wound stitched.

He went back into the bedroom, opened his suitcase and took out the well-equipped medical kit he always travelled with. He ripped the sterilized wrapping off a field dressing and taped it firmly to his side. After waiting a half hour to make sure that the bleeding had stopped he took two penicillin tablets and a valium and went to bed. '*Bitch*,' he muttered under his breath before he fell asleep.

When Makepeace emerged from her bedroom at just after 7 a.m. Dempsey was already up and drinking a cup of coffee. She was concerned at how haggard he looked. 'How do you feel?' she asked worriedly.

'Better on seeing you,' he said with a grin. 'That's quite a nice little number you're wearing.' He was referring to her translucent Japanese-style dressing gown. It left little to the imagination but she had put it on automatically, forgetting that

Dempsey was in the flat.

She frowned and pulled the sheer red silk tighter around her — a futile gesture, really, as she was wearing nothing beneath it — and crossed her arms. Dempsey's grin grew broader. 'You look terrible,' she told him accusingly. 'Didn't you sleep?'

'Not much,' he admitted. 'Damn neck kept me awake. It's as stiff as hell. And when I did sleep I had bad dreams. Nightmares. The kind of ones I used to have as a kid. About the Bogeyman.'

'The Bogeyman?'

'A guy in black. Used to chase me down a long corridor. There was a door at the end of it but I could never reach it. The faster I ran the further away it got. But everytime I looked over my shoulder the Bogeyman was closer. Reaching out for me.' Dempsey ran a hand over his unshaven chin. 'Haven't had that dream since I was about twelve years old — until last night. Funny thing was I was a kid again . . .'

He got up and went to the window. It was raining and everything outside looked grey. 'Jesus, this weather. I don't know how you put up with it. Even New York's weather is better than this.' He sighed. 'Maybe I'm getting homesick . . . maybe that's what's wrong with me . . .'

'I think you should take the day off today. Go back to your flat and get some rest. Or stay here if you like,' Makepeace offered.

He turned to her. 'Nah, princess. I've got to get the Bogeyman. Before he gets *me* . . .'

Chapter SIX

Lymon was pacing up and down in Rose's office like a caged animal. An angry caged animal. Rose, seated behind his desk, watched him warily, a benign smile fixed securely on his round face. 'You certainly were lucky last night,' he told Lymon for at least the third time.

Lymon swore, 'The bastard. I still can't figure out how he found out about old Kelly.'

'Like I said, people talk,' Rose shrugged. 'This cop probably paid a visit to some of your regular haunts and asked a few questions.'

'But I don't *have* any regular haunts,' protested Lymon.

'You sure about that?'

'Yeah ...' Lymon paused. 'Well, there's the Beckett but the cop *couldn't* have known about that.'

'Don't underestimate cops, lad. Especially this one. He's obviously pretty sharp. So far you've led a charmed life as far as the cops are concerned but now the situation has changed. This Yank is out to get you.'

'Bleeding Yank,' snarled Lymon. It's *my* country. What's he doin' here anyway?'

Rose shrugged. 'Search me. The problem is he's here and he wants you.'

'I've handled cops before.'

'This isn't just police. This is S.I.10. That's a firm within a firm. They operate by their own rules and they play hard. Real hard.'

'Bastards,' said Lymon bitterly.

'Well, sure they are. But somehow they got you targetted. So why don't you go away somewhere and lay low. Somewhere like Spain. Wait until they've forgotten about you. Moved onto something else . . .'

'Hold the phone — what am I gonna do in Spain!' cried Lymon. 'I live here! This is my patch, not bloody Spain!'

Rose continued on calmly, using his most persuasive tone of voice, 'If you need any bread I'll see you right. I've got contacts in Spain. They'll look after you. When I want to be paid back I'll bring you over for a job. You don't like the job you don't owe me. Now what could be fairer than that?' Rose leaned back in his chair and lit a cigarette.

Lymon stopped his pacing and faced Rose. 'I ain't running from no Yank.'

'Nicky lad, this Yank's too close for comfort. He's going to get you if you stay in England.'

'No he ain't. Nobody gets to me. Nobody.'

Rose regarded him sadly. 'Whatever you say. But as long as S.I.10 has you marked don't ask me for a job. Right?'

'I ain't asking you for a job.'

'No?' Rose couldn't help looking relieved.

'No.' Lymon leaned on Rose's desk. In a calm, cold voice he said, 'I'm *telling* you to get me one. And fast.'

'Oh yes?' said Rose uneasily. 'And if I don't?'

'I'll blow you away.' He smiled grimly. 'Know what I mean?'

Rose choked on his cigarette. When he'd finished coughing he said, 'Look, I just can't conjure up a job out of thin air. It takes time. A lot of research is involved. Checking schedules and double-checking. Surveillance work and all that.'

'I'll give you a week. You don't have a job for me then I'll blow your fat belly all over the wall.'

'A *week*. But . . .'

'A week. And there's something else I want you to do for me.'

'Yes?' said Rose weakly.

'I want a place to hole up in. Someplace safe and secure. Fix it *now*.'

Rose looked even more worried. 'Well, I got a place over a record shop in Old Compton Street but I'm renting that out to a mate of mine . . .'

'Get him out. Today.'

'But I can't just tell him to . . .'

'*Today*,' repeated Lymon coldly.

Rose swallowed and nodded. 'Whatever you say, Nicky. Whatever you say . . .'

The killer woke at 8 a.m. and examined his wound. There had been little bleeding during the night. It felt sore and his ribs ached but he felt confident it would give him no further trouble providing he gave it at least a couple of days to heal. He was annoyed at this further complication to the assignment but he was determined that his third attempt to kill Dempsey would be successful. His professional pride was at stake. It had become more than just another contract — it was personal now.

'So you let him slip through your fingers *again*,' growled Spikings.

Dempsey bristled. 'You don't have to rub it in, chief. I feel bad enough as it is.'

'It wasn't Dempsey's fault, sir,' Makepeace said quickly. 'He had no idea that there was a second man lying in wait for him. He had no reason to . . .'

Spikings scowled. 'So who the hell is this "Mystery Man" of yours? How does he fit into the scheme of things?'

'Bogeyman,' muttered Dempsey, almost to himself. 'We call him the Bogeyman.'

'What?!' demanded Spikings, staring at him.

'Nothing.'

'Dempsey, are you feeling all right? You look half-dead.

'I'm fine, sir.'

'You sure about that? I don't want you fouling things up just because you're too proud to admit you're not feeling a hundred percent. Any member of S.I.10 who can't pull his weight is a danger to his colleagues as well as to himself.'

'I know, sir,' said Dempsey stiffly. 'You don't have to worry on that score.'

'I hope not. So what have you got on this, this *Bogeyman* . . .?' Spikings' lip curled with disgust at the word.

'Just this.' Dempsey produced the flat-bladed throwing knife that had narrowly missed Makepeace.

'The forensic guys checked it out. No prints. No manufacturer's trademark either. It's a hand-tooled job.'

Spikings reached over and took the knife. 'Nasty,' he said as he examined it. 'So our mystery man rolls his own, does he? Interesting.' He gave the knife back to Dempsey.

'It suggests he's serious about his work. Very serious,' said Makepeace. 'And that fits my theory that he's a professional hit-man. Someone Miller hired to do in Dempsey.'

Spikings looked thoughtful. 'We got anyone on our files that fits this profile? An expert knife-thrower? Knows karate? Good with a rifle?'

'No,' admitted Dempsey.

'Which means he was brought in from outside the country,' said Makepeace.

'Doesn't sound like Miller's way of doing things,' said Spikings doubtfully. 'Be more in his style just to hire a few cheap East End heavies to lay in wait for you.'

'Can you think of another explanation?' Makepeace asked him.

He glowered at her. 'Not right now, no. But he's not our main priority at the moment. Getting Nicky Lymon *is*. So what's your next step?'

'The trail's gone cold,' admitted Dempsey. 'We've grilled the old guy — Kelly — but he says he has no idea where Lymon might have gone after leaving his place, and I believe him.'

'Surely he must know the names of Lymon's friends? He's got to be hiding out with somebody!'

'According to old Kelly, Lymon doesn't have any friends, which is not exactly a surprise. The guy's a loner.'

Spikings thumped the desk with the palm of his hand. 'This isn't good enough. The man is not only a menace to society he's left S.I.10 looking stupid, thanks to *you*, Dempsey! I want him and I want him *today*!'

Back in their office Dempsey looked at Makepeace and said, 'Any ideas?'

''Nary a one. What we need is a miracle.'

It was just then that Dempsey's phone rang. He picked it up and said listlessly, 'Yeah?'

'Lieutenant Dempsey?' asked a nervous-sounding voice on the other end of the line.

'You got him. What can I do for you?'

'It's more a case of what I can do for you, Lieutenant.'

'Yeah?'

'It concerns Nick Lymon.'

Dempsey sat bolt upright in his chair. 'Who are you?' he asked eagerly.

'I'd prefer to remain anonymous for reasons of . . . er, health. I'm sure you can appreciate my position.'

'You know where Lymon is?'

At the mention of Lymon's name Makepeace gave him an enquiring glance but he ignored her, his attention completely focussed on the voice at the other end of the line.

'I know exactly where he is.'

'So tell me!'

'First I want your assurance that, if he survives, you won't tell him you found out where he was through a tip-off. If you do he's sure to realize where it came from and I'm done for.'

'Listen,' said Dempsey, 'I get my hands on Lymon and you got no worries on that score. By the time he gets out of prison Halley's comet will be making a return visit.'

The man gave a bitter laugh and said, 'No offence, Lieutenant, but from what I know of Lymon, keeping him behind bars is not going to be easy. I don't want to wake up one morning and find him at the bottom of my bed. So you got to promise me you'll come up with a good explanation for how you ran him down. No mention of any tip-off, right?'

'You got it,' agreed Dempsey. 'Now give me the address.'

The man did so. Dempsey quickly jotted it down. Then he asked, 'What's the best way into the place?'

'Sorry. I've been talking long enough. From now on you are on your own. Just make sure you get him — for all our sakes.' There was a click and the line went dead.

As Rose put the phone down he realized he was shaking. He stared at his trembling hand with a growing feeling of resentment. How dare a punk kid like Lymon throw this kind of scare into him! He was Harry Rose. He'd been dealing with trash like Lymon for over twenty years . . .

Well . . . he had to admit he'd never encountered anyone *quite* like Lymon before. The kid was a psycho. You could sense the built-up rage inside him. Anything could set him off. Anything at all. And he'd kill you without a second's hesitation.

He shuddered at the thought of what would happen if Lymon even suspected that he had tipped off Dempsey. Quickly he pulled open a drawer in his desk and took out a bottle of Bells whisky. He had to drink the equivalent of six doubles before the shaking in his hands stopped.

'We just got our miracle, princess,' said Dempsey, showing Makepeace the address.

'Lymon?'

He nodded, looking thoughtful.

'You don't seem very pleased.'

'The trouble is I don't believe in miracles. It just seems too easy, being handed Lymon on a plate.'

'Well, there's still the difficult bit of actually *taking* him,' she pointed out. 'It's not what I would describe as being handed Lymon on a plate. All we've been told is where he is.'

'*If* the guy was telling the truth.'

'You think it might be a set-up?'

'It's a possibility. I mean, why would this guy want to turn Lymon in?'

'Good taste?' suggested Makepeace.

He scowled at her. 'Maybe the guy on the phone was our Man in Black. He could be trying to get another crack at me.'

Makepeace considered this and nodded. 'But there's an easy solution to that possibility. You just stay here and let the rest of us carry out the grab.'

'No way,' said Dempsey firmly. 'Lymon is *my* pigeon. Set-up or no set-up, I'm gonna be there.'

'If you insist.'

'I insist.' He got to his feet. 'Come on, let's go see Spikings and organize a raiding party.'

Chapter SEVEN

'So here's the situation,' said Dempsey, pointing at the blackboard in the S.I.10 briefing room. 'This is the flat on the first floor. There's only one entrance. Up these stairs at the side of the record shop. But there's a fire-escape at the rear — here — which is accessible via the kitchen window here . . .' Dempsey moved the pointer to indicate the window concerned. The diagram had been put together by Phil and another S.I.10 man who had surreptitiously checked out the address that afternoon.

'Now I want that rear exit well and truly covered,' continued Dempsey. 'I want a man on the roof in case he decides to go up, and I want two men waiting at the bottom of the fire escape if he goes the other way. Dave, Roy and Peter, you handle that side.' The three men nodded. Phil spoke up, 'What about me?'

'You'll be with me and Makepeace going in the

front way. That all right with you?'

'Sure,' said Phil, but without enthusiasm.

'Now we know the guy has a shotgun but he might have got his hands on other weapons by now. And there's also the possibility that the other guy — our Mystery Man with the rifle — might be in the vicinity. So we're going in with these babies . . .' Dempsey held up a compact, angular sub-machine gun. 'I know some of you are familiar with this weapon but for those who're not I'll give you a quick briefing. This is a Uzi sub-machine gun, named after the man who invented it, Major Uzi Gal of the Israeli army. It fires 9mm parabellum bullets at a rate of six hundred and fifty a minute and at a velocity of thirteen hundred and ten feet per second. Its detachable staggered-box magazine has three separate load capacities. It also has a slide selector switch which permits single action or fully automatic bursts . . .'

Dempsey demonstrated the switch on the side of the gun. Then he went on: 'The Uzi has almost no recoil and only weighs eight point eight pounds when fully loaded. It's also very easy to conceal under clothing . . . like this . . .' Dempsey hid the gun under his left arm inside his coat jacket. 'Which is one of the reasons we'll be carrying them tonight. Now when this briefing is over I want each of you to go practise with one of these in the firing range. Any questions?'

One of the S.I.10 men, Dave Barnes, asked, 'Have we got permission to be packing so much firepower?'

Dempsey glanced at Chas who confirmed, 'Chief Superintendent Spikings has got a special dispensation from the Home Office.'

'What about the boys from West End Central?' asked Phil. 'They're going to be pissed off if we have a fire fight in the middle of their patch.'

'They've been informed that we will be carrying out an operation in Soho tonight,' Chas told him. 'Their brass aren't happy about it, of course, but then they've never liked us. Can't imagine why.'

This drew a few chuckles. Then Dempsey said, 'I sure as hell hope we *don't* have a fire fight. My aim is to nab Lymon quickly and cleanly without any gun-play. If we can take him by surprise there shouldn't be any problem. Trouble is there are a couple of unknown factors loose in the works. One is that Lymon is unpredictable — we know that from yesterday morning's show — the other is the mystery guy who seemed to be shadowing Lymon last night . . .'

'The Bogeyman,' murmured Makepeace.

The others all looked at her questioningly. Dempsey scowled.

'It's our code word for him,' she said quickly. 'Isn't it, Lieutenant?'

Dempsey had no choice but to nod reluctantly.

'How ya doin', kid?' Dempsey asked Phil, having noticed the younger man looking distinctly uneasy.

'Okay.'

They were sitting in a car parked in Old Compton Street. Almost directly opposite was the record shop. In exactly ten minutes it would be time to move in.

'It's gonna be a cinch,' Dempsey told Phil.

'Yeah, I know.' Phil kept staring about restlessly, peering intently into the faces of passers-by. Even though it was nearly midnight there were still a lot of pedestrians about.

'Look, all you have to do is cover me,' said Dempsey. '*I'll* be the one going through the door first.'

'Hey, I'm okay, *really*,' said Phil with a touch of irritation. This only made Dempsey more dubious about him. He was beginning to think that Phil wasn't suitable material for S.I.10. Depending on how he behaved during the operation itself he might have to have a talk with Spikings and suggest a transfer . . .

'Here's the Sergeant,' said Phil suddenly.

Dempsey looked and couldn't help smiling. Makepeace, in a black wig, dark glasses, red leather mini skirt and black fish-net stockings was masquerading, against her wishes, as a hooker.

She opened the rear door of the car and climbed in. 'No sign of our Bogeyman,' she said, taking off the wig and shaking her blonde hair. 'Couldn't spot anyone on any of the roofs around here. And the only people lurking suspiciously about are the people who *always* lurk suspiciously about in this area.'

Dempsey leaned over the back of his seat and grinned at her. 'Get any offers of business?'

She was slipping into a long, dark coat. Coldly, she said, 'If I'd accepted all the offers I've received during the last thirty minutes I could retire from the Force tomorrow and go and live in the South of France.'

'In that case maybe you should think seriously about doin' some moonlighting.'

She curled her upper lip at him.

Phil said tensely, 'Two minutes to go.'

'Right,' said Dempsey. He opened a case at his feet and produced three Uzis. He handed one to Makepeace and another to Phil. 'Make sure they're cocked the way I showed you . . .'

Almost simultaneously there was the sound of two bolts being pulled back. Dempsey cocked his own weapon then looked at his watch. 'The others will be in position so let's move.'

Dempsey led the way across the street. He couldn't help imagining that there was a rifle sight trained on his back. If Makepeace hadn't spotted anyone on a roof he was ninety-nine percent certain the mystery gunman wasn't around but it was the remaining one percent of doubt that made him nervous. With every step he expected to feel a bullet come smashing into him . . .

He gave an inward sigh of relief when he reached the shelter of the open doorway beside the record shop. He looked up the narrow flight of stairs lit by a single bare light bulb. There was no one in sight. He removed the Uzi from inside his jacket. Makepeace and Phil did likewise.

As quietly as he could he climbed the old wooden stairs. Phil was directly behind him and Makepeace brought up the rear as per the plan. She, Dempsey knew, would be checking the street doorway to make sure no one caught them by surprise from that direction.

When he reached the tiny landing Dempsey looked at his watch again. Zero hour. 'Here I go . . .' he whispered.

He launched himself at the door, delivering a massive kick to the lock with the heel of his right boot. Wood splintered and the door flew open. He dived through the doorway, the Uzi held in one hand. He hit the floor and rolled, then sprung up yelling, 'Police, Lymon! Don't move . . .!'

The combined bedroom and sitting room was in darkness but there was enough light from the landing to show that the bed was empty. Dempsey swivelled, looking for his target, but a glance was enough to tell him the room was empty as well.

As Phil and Makepeace entered behind him, he cried, 'Phil, the bathroom!' Then, in a low crouch, he sprang into the kitchen. That too was empty. He stood up and turned on the light. The kitchen window that led out onto the fire escape was shut. He heard Phil call, 'No one here, Lieutenant!'

'*Damn and hell*,' muttered Dempsey. He went to the window and raised it. There was no sign of anyone on the fire escape. He poked his head out and called, 'Dave! You see anyone?!'

'No one, Lieutenant!' came the answer from above.

'Roy? Peter?'

'Same here!' was the reply from the base of the fire-escape.

Cursing, Dempsey returned to the main room. He saw that Phil was looking as tense as ever, his eyes darting all around the room. Makepeace, on the other hand, just looked disappointed. 'After we've gone to all this trouble for him you'd think the sod would have at least been at home when we arrived,' she said with a wry smile.

Dempsey looked puzzled. 'I can't figure out what Lymon would be doing out when he's . . .'

He never got to finish the sentence. Without warning Phil opened fire with his Uzi, spraying a small cupboard near Makepeace with bullets. To Dempsey's horror she gave a cry of pain. She'd been hit . . .!

With a bellow of rage Dempsey leapt forward and knocked Phil's Uzi upwards so that the rest of the burst went into the ceiling. 'Have you gone crazy!!' he yelled, grabbing Phil by his jacket lapels and throwing him across the room. Then he turned to Makepeace. She was clutching her left arm. Blood was seeping through her jacket sleeve just above the elbow. Her face was white with shock.

'Princess . . .?'

'I'm okay.' She managed a strained smile. 'I think it's only a flesh wound, as they say in the movies.'

'Let me take a look,' he ordered. He helped her off with the jacket then ripped open the sleeve of her blouse. He wiped away the blood with his handkerchief and examined the wound. He was relieved to see it was nothing serious. The bullet had just nicked the flesh on her upper arm. To hide his true feelings he said roughly, 'You're right. Nothing more than a scratch.' Then he used a strip of her torn sleeve to make a temporary bandage.

By now the other three S.I.10 men had arrived via the kitchen window. 'What happened?' asked Dave Barnes, staring at Makepeaces's arm. 'Did Lymon . . .?'

'No, it wasn't Lymon,' growled Dempsey, jerking his thumb at Phil who sat slumped in a chair. 'It was Dillinger over there, shooting at shadows.' He turned to Phil, 'Just what the hell were you playing at, letting off a burst like that when one of your partners is practically in your line of fire.'

Phil pointed at the bullet-riddled cupboard door. 'I saw it move. I thought Lymon might be . . .'

'In there?' Dempsey asked sarcastically. He went over to the cupboard and opened the door. The interior, which was only about three feet high and two and a half feet wide, was crammed with old magazines. 'Lymon's not a bloody midget, you know,' said Dempsey.

Phil covered his face with his hand. 'I'm sorry.'

'*You're* sorry? Another few inches and Sergeant Makepeace here would be checking in at the nearest morgue for the night!'

'Take it easy, Dempsey,' said Makepeace quietly. 'Phil is obviously feeling more shaken up about it than I am. What we should be talking about right now is Lymon.'

Dempsey's shoulders sagged. 'Yeah, you're right. As I was saying before we were so rudely interrupted,' — he shot a contemptuous glance at Phil — 'I can't figure out why Lymon would be out and about. He must know every cop in London has seen his picture. Anyone in his position would be lying low in this apartment . . .'

'You said he was unpredictable,' Makepeace pointed out.

'Yeah,' agreed Dempsey. 'Maybe he just doesn't give a damn, the arrogant son-of-a-bitch. Or maybe whoever tipped us off was playing us for suckers.'

'What do we do now?' asked Dave Barnes.

Dempsey gloomily surveyed the wreckage of the front door. 'No way we can pretend we haven't been here. If Lymon comes back he's gonna see that mess when he's halfway up the stairs. I guess all we can do is stake out the street and grab him as soon as he goes in the front entrance. *If* he comes back, that is.' He turned to Phil who was still sitting slumped in the chair. 'You feel fit enough to drive?'

'Yeah,' said Phil. He didn't look up.

'Then drive the Sergeant to the infirmary. When they've patched her up drive her home, then go home yourself. I'll talk to you tomorrow . . .'

Phil nodded and rose slowly to his feet. Makepeace said, 'Look, Dempsey, I'm fine. I can stick it out to the end of the operation.'

Dempsey shook his head. 'You're going now. No arguments. I'm running this show and you'll do as I say.'

She could tell by the tone of his voice that it would be futile trying to argue with him so she picked up her coat and said, 'Come on, Phil. Let's go. Good luck, everybody.'

Phil followed her out without saying anything.

When they'd gone Dempsey said, 'Okay, first thing we do is search this place for weapons. I'll feel a lot happier if I find Lymon's shotgun here . . .'

But the shotgun wasn't in the flat, it was in the cloth bag hanging from Lymon's shoulder. Lymon himself was standing in a shop doorway nearby in Old Compton Street. He had been there for the last fifteen minutes when he had spotted Dempsey, Makepeace and a third familiar figure heading towards the entrance to his flat beside the record shop.

Now he watched Makepeace and the other man emerge and get into their car. The Yank didn't appear, which meant he was still in the flat.

Lymon fingered the shotgun through the cloth of the bag and considered his next move.

Chapter EIGHT

Harry Rose had smoked so many cigarettes during the last few hours that a smoggy haze filled his office. He stubbed out a butt and looked again at his watch. Surely they'd picked up Lymon by now. But he'd wait awhile before he called Dempsey to make sure. Give him time to get back to S.I.10 headquarters with his catch . . .

He lit another cigarette and took yet another swallow from the nearly empty whisky bottle. What if something had gone wrong, he asked himself nervously? What if Lymon had got away? He'd know for sure it was Rose who'd turned him in . . .

His office door opened. He knew he'd locked it but it opened anyway.

Lymon entered.

Rose stared at him in disbelief.

'You're working late, Harry,' said Lymon quietly.

'What — what are you doing here?' Rose stammered.

Lymon pulled over a chair and sat down. He put his cloth bag across his lap. Rose could see the outline of the shotgun. He felt as if someone had just injected a massive amount of icy cold water into his lower bowel. He wanted to run but all he could do was sit there behind his desk and stare at Lymon like a rabbit hypnotized by a snake.

'Had a bit of bother tonight,' said Lymon in the same quiet tones.

'Bother? What kind of bother?' Rose tried but couldn't keep the tremor from his voice.

'That place you fixed for me. It got raided. By that big Yank and his friends.'

'Raided?' Rose sucked on his cigarette as if he was an oxygen-starved diver and it was an air tube. 'You're kidding!'

'Straight up. Less than half an hour ago.' Lymon kept his eyes on Rose's face. His own face was expressionless.

'How — how did you get away?'

'I wasn't in the flat. Just comin' back from that drinking club in Denmark Street and I spotted them movin' in.'

'You were *out*!' exclaimed Rose. 'But — but that was a crazy thing to do! There's an APB out on you! Your face was on the front page of the *Standard* tonight. You could have been spotted!'

'So I took a risk. I don't like being cooped up. And anyway, if I'd stayed in I'd have got nicked, wouldn't I?'

Rose swallowed. 'Yeah, that's true . . .'

After a long pause, Lymon said pleasantly, 'Funny, innit, how the filth knew I was stayin' at that place.

Hadn't even been there a day.'

Rose was now experiencing severe stomach cramps. He badly wanted to go to the toilet. He wondered when Lymon would stop this playing about and blow him away with the shotgun. 'You don't — you don't think *I* tipped them off do you?' he asked weakly.

A look of mild surprise appeared on Lymon's face. '*You*? 'Course not. You wouldn't do a thing like that, would you?'

'No, no, never!' agreed Rose quickly.

'I mean, we're partners after all.'

'Yes. Yes! Partners!' Rose jumped as the cigarette burned his fingers. He hastily stubbed it out and lit another one. He was daring to feel relieved. He knew that Lymon knew he had tipped off Dempsey but for reasons of his own Lymon wasn't going to kill him — yet. Those reasons became clear with Lymon's next words.

'I mean, you're going to fix me up with a nice little earner, ain't you?'

'Right! In fact I got wind of a job today that might be exactly what you're looking for. I'm going to get the details tomorrow.'

'Good,' smiled Lymon. He leaned back in the chair and said, 'What I expect happened was that someone spotted me movin' into that place this afternoon. Like you said, my face is plastered everywhere.'

Rose nodded eagerly, happy to play along with the charade, 'Yeah, that's it! Some uniformed copper on the beat, most likely.'

'Trouble is,' said Lymon. 'I'm out of a place to stay again, ain't I. Which is why I came to see you.'

Rose frowned. 'I don't have any other flats, Nicky. Sorry, I just can't help you . . .'

'Then I'll move in with you,' said Lymon casually.

'*What*!?' yelped Rose.

'No problem, is there?'

Rose had been caught completely off-guard. 'No — no, it's just that my old lady, Beth, doesn't know about what I, you know, er, *do*. On the side, I mean. So it would be rather inconvenient for you to stay there . . .'

'Just tell her I'm a client of yours you're helpin' out,' said Lymon with a shrug.

'No, you don't know Beth. It wouldn't work.' He shook his head. 'No, sorry, it's not on. We'll have to think of something else . . .'

Lymon ran his fingers along the shotgun in the bag. Coldly, he said, 'It *is* on, mate. Sod your inconvenience. Sod your old woman as well. I'm movin' in with you. For the duration. Until I carry out this job you're gonna fix up for me, I want to be where I can keep an eye on you. Know what I mean?'

'Yeah,' said Rose hoarsely, 'I know what you mean.'

Spikings did not look happy. On the contrary he looked like a volcano with indigestion. Dempsey was wondering how long it would be before the eruption.

'So what do you think went wrong?' asked Spikings in a dangerously low voice.

Dempsey spread his hands. 'Coulda been a number of things. Either it was a set-up or Lymon had already moved on. We staked out the place all night but he never showed. I still got a couple of the guys keeping watch but I don't think he'll show now.'

'What about the owner of the flat. Any luck tracking down his name?'

'Nope. Place is owned by a company. A dummy company. No clue as to who's behind it.'

Spikings scowled. 'You seem to be under some kind of jinx when it comes to this Lymon character.'

'Jinx or not I'll get him, Chief.'

Spikings didn't look convinced by Dempsey's pledge. 'If you don't make some progress soon I'll hand the operation to someone else.'

'I'd appreciate it if you didn't, sir,' said Dempsey grimly.

'We'll see. How's Makepeace?'

'Fine. Wound only needed a couple of stitches. She'll be in this morning. I told her to take the day off but she insisted.'

Spikings gave a non-committal grunt. Then, 'It was a close shave for her.'

'A *very* close shave,' agreed Dempsey.

'Bloody Phil. He's finished with S.I.10, of course.'

Dempsey nodded. 'I guessed he would be. You want to tell him or should I?'

'*I'll* tell him,' said Spikings with relish. 'I'll make sure he ends up back on the beat.'

Dempsey said nothing. He felt a certain amount of sympathy for Phil but he knew he'd never be able to forgive him for almost killing Makepeace.

'Your mystery man didn't show up either last night?' asked Spikings.

'Nope. Not a sign of him.'

Spikings slammed his hand down on his desk. 'This can't go on, Dempsey! I'm not having it! Lymon and this other gunman running around loose and us twiddling our thumbs when we're not taking pot-shots at each other!'

'How do you think *I* feel, Chief?' said Dempsey stiffly.

'I don't *care* how you feel!!' thundered Spikings. 'I just want this case wrapped up!! As soon as possible, or you'll find yourself on a plane back to New York!!'

When Dempsey got back to the outer office he found Makepeace there talking to Chas. She looked paler than usual but otherwise fine.

'How ya feeling?' he asked roughly.

'Okay. Arm's a little sore, that's all. How about you? How's the neck?'

'Still pretty stiff,' he admitted, giving the large bruise on the side of his neck a brief rub.

'At least you've still got your head on your shoulders,' said Chas. 'From the sound of it the Chief was carrying out a public execution just then.'

'Yeah,' admitted Dempsey ruefully. 'Threatened to ship me back to the States. I think he wants me on one plane and my ass on another . . .'

In his car parked a couple of blocks away the killer frowned when he heard these words through his receiver. It would be awkward for all concerned if Dempsey got back to New York. Somehow he had to dispose of him very quickly. But how?

Cautiously, he touched the wound in his side. It was healing but it was still painful. It would be at least another day before he could be sure that any strenuous activity wouldn't open it up again.

He sighed. If only he could come up with a scheme to eliminate Dempsey that would also include his bitch of a partner.

The killer smiled at the thought

'So what do we do now?' Makepeace asked Dempsey.

'Good question. All we can hope is that the guy who tipped us off yesterday gives us another call.'

'But we don't know if that was a genuine tip-off,' she pointed out.

'Yeah,' admitted Dempsey wearily. 'Hell, I'd give anything to know who that guy is and why he's mixed up with Lymon.'

Harry Rose, at that moment, would have given anything to be anywhere but in his kitchen having breakfast with his mistress, Beth, and Lymon.

The atmosphere in the kitchen was oppressive. Beth, a plump, blonde woman in her early forties, had made it perfectly clear that she couldn't stand Lymon and wanted him out of the house. Harry had tried to explain to her that Lymon was very important to him and that it was in both their best interests that she shouldn't be rude to him. But this plea had fallen on deaf ears. Ever since Lymon had got up she had been making increasingly sarcastic remarks about him and Rose could see that Lymon was beginning to get annoyed . . .

'Harry dear, would you mind asking your *guest* if he wouldn't mind eating with his mouth shut,' she said, as Lymon consumed his fourth fried egg in a spectacularly messy fashion.

Lymon looked at her, then looked at Harry. Harry winced and said, 'Please dear . . .'

She slammed her coffee cup down on its saucer and stood up. 'I'm going to have my bath,' she informed Harry and marched out of the kitchen.

'What's her problem?' Lymon asked Harry.

'Well, Nick, she sort of regards this house as her private kingdom. Very fussy, she is. And you being a stranger . . .'

'She's a stuck-up cow,' said Lymon coldly, 'She keeps pulling my string I'll lay one on her.'

Harry winced again. The image of Lymon punching Beth in the nose sprang to his mind with a dreadful clarity. 'I'll talk to her again.'

'You do that,' said Lymon, spreading a great dollop of jam over a piece of toast. After taking a couple of huge bites out of it, and dripping jam on the tablecloth in the process, Lymon said, through a mouthful of toast, 'She your wife?'

'Oh no,' said Harry, shaking his head. 'I left my wife when I met Beth. That was nearly ten years ago.'

'Ten years. And in all that time the silly cow has never found out you're a villain?'

'No.'

'She thinks you get the money to pay for all this —', he waved the piece of toast to indicate the size of the well-equipped kitchen and the rest of the house, '— from that third-rate agency you operate?'

'Well, yes . . .'

'She must be really dense.'

'Well, we never really discuss money much . . .'

'You just give it to her.'

Harry nodded.

Lymon grinned at him. It was a very malign grin. 'You keep her on her leash then or I'll start tellin' her some things about you.'

'Don't, please.'

'No more lip from her or else.'

'I'll make it clear to her, don't worry,' Harry assured him though he had no idea how he was going to make Beth see reason.

'We gonna have that cow on our necks all day?'

'Oh no,' said Harry. 'I set her up in a hairdressing business in the Fulham Road. She'll be off to it soon. Likes to make sure her staff are in on time.'

Lymon nodded. He lit a cigarette. Harry had to stop himself from saying that Beth didn't allow smoking in the kitchen. Lymon said, 'This job you said you got wind of . . .?'

'It's another security van job.'

'It had better work better than your last one.'

'Nothing will go wrong, I promise you.'

Lymon smiled his malign smile again.

Harry was waiting in the bedroom when Beth emerged from the bathroom. Before she had a chance to open her mouth he gripped her by the arms, hard, and said in a low, angry voice, 'Beth, listen to me. No more insults to Lymon. Promise me! Otherwise you're going to put me in a whole lot of trouble. *Big* trouble!'

Beth looked at him in surprise. He'd never talked to her like that before. 'But the man's an animal. I don't want him in my house a minute longer!'

'It's not your house, *I* paid for it,' he said brutally. 'And if you don't start being pleasant to Lymon I'm going to have no choice but to kick you out.'

Her mouth dropped open with astonishment. 'But you wouldn't! You couldn't!'

'I don't want to but I will if you don't do as I say.' He gave her a hard shake to emphasize his point.

Puzzlement appeared in her eyes, as well as alarm.

'Who *is* that man? Why should one of your clients have such a hold on you?'

He sighed. 'I can't explain right now. Just do as I say and don't ask questions. It won't be for long. He'll be gone in a few days.'

'No, I can't take any more of him . . .'

Rose released his grip on her left arm and slapped her hard across the face. She gave a cry and tried to pull away from him. He slapped her again. 'Will you do as I say?' He shook her then raised his right hand again.

Speechless with shock, and with her eyes filling with tears, she nodded.

When Beth had left for work he rang his contact in the security van company. The man, who was on his day off, gave him the relevant details. Rose agreed on a payment when the job had been pulled off successfully then hung up. He turned to Lymon who was watching him intently. 'It's looking good,' he told him. 'Should go like a dream.' He then repeated the details to Lymon who nodded approvingly. 'Yeah, I'll buy that,' he said. 'There'd just better not be any foul-ups this time. I smell any trouble, I not only blow you away but your old lady as well. Know what I mean?'

'There won't be any foul-ups, Nick. I keep telling you that.'

Later in the morning Lymon said he wanted to borrow Rose's car as he had some business to take care of. Rose wasn't happy about the idea of Lymon driving his car around but he knew it would be futile to try and argue with him.

When Lymon had gone Rose poured himself a stiff

scotch and sat down in his favourite armchair. He looked at the problem from all angles but there was only one possible answer. He had no choice.

He finished the whisky, got up and went to the phone. He dialled a number then said, 'Give me Lieutenant Dempsey . . .'

Chapter NINE

'You're the guy who called yesterday,' said Dempsey, signalling at the same time to Makepeace to patch her own phone into the line.

'That's right.'

'So what went wrong? We were there, Lymon wasn't.'

'He was out having a drink. He spotted you moving in just as he was coming back. You missed him by seconds.'

'Damn,' muttered Dempsey. 'Do you know where he is now?'

'Unfortunately, yes.'

'Give.'

'First I want to make a deal.'

'No deals,' said Dempsey.

'Then no Lymon.'

Stalemate, thought Dempsey angrily. 'Don't hang

up! Maybe we can sort something out.'

'If you want Lymon you're going to have to make a deal. You do want him, don't you?'

'Yeah, I want him,' said Dempsey grimly.

'So we talk a deal?'

After a long pause Dempsey sighed and said, 'Yeah, we talk a deal. What do you want?'

'Not over the phone. We meet somewhere. Today.'

'Where?' asked Dempsey, suspiciously.

'Hampstead Heath. By the Highgate Ponds. Know where they are?'

'No. But I'll find out.'

'I'll meet you there at one sharp. But you must promise to come alone.'

'Okay. But how'll I know you?'

'I'll be the fat man feeding the ducks. Remember, come alone. And no tricks.' Then the phone went dead.

Dempsey hung up and looked at Makepeace. 'What do you think?'

'I don't like it,' she said. 'Could be a set-up.'

'Yeah. But I got to take that risk.'

'I'll come with you but I'll stay out of sight.'

He shook his head. 'No, princess,' he said firmly. 'Can't take the chance of scaring him off if he is on the level.'

'Dempsey, don't be silly,' she said angrily. 'You're going to need a back-up.'

'No. I'm gonna do this my way.' He grinned at her. 'Don't worry. I'll be careful.'

Makepeace didn't reply but her expression made it clear she wasn't reassured.

It was a cold day and there weren't many people on

the Heath as Dempsey made his way to the Highgate Ponds. As he walked he warily scanned his surroundings. He knew Makepeace was right — he *was* taking an awful risk. He felt too exposed, too vulnerable, but as he'd said to her he had no choice. He *had* to do it if there was even a remote chance it would lead to Lymon . . .

As he got nearer to the Ponds he spotted his contact: a fat man in a heavy overcoat who was feeding the ducks. There was no one else in the vicinity.

Dempsey went and stood five or six feet away from him and pretended to take an interest in the ducks.

'You Dempsey?' asked the fat man.

'Who else?'

The fat man looked around nervously. 'You alone?'

'I said I would be, so I am.'

'If I find you're lying to me the deal's off.'

'I'm not lying,' said Dempsey. 'Believe me, Mister . . .?'

'No, you're not getting my name. Not yet, anyway.'

'What *am* I gonna get?'

'Lymon, of course.'

'How can I trust you?' Dempsey asked him. 'You're mixed up with him in some way so why are you playing the stool pigeon?'

The fat man reached into his coat pocket and pulled out another handful of bread crumbs. He threw them into the water. The ducks competed noisily for the food. 'I'm "mixed up" with him as you say, yeah, but not willingly. I'll tell you frankly he scares the hell out of me. And I know he's going to kill me. He knows I tipped you off yesterday.'

'Why hasn't he killed you already then?'

'He needs me.'

Dempsey glanced at him. 'Needs you? How?'

'All in good time, Lieutenant. After we make our deal.'

'I know what I want. What do *you* want?'

'Two things. Obviously the first is that I want Lymon off my back. The second is that I want a promise of immunity from prosecution.'

'That's a tall order,' said Dempsey.

'You can swing it. Or rather your superiors can. I know all about S.I.10. It doesn't just bend the rules, it drives straight through them.'

'Even if something could be arranged — and it's a *big* if — I want to know first what you've done that you don't want to be prosecuted for.'

'It's not so much what I've done — it's what I'm going to do.'

Dempsey gave him a puzzled look. 'You've lost me, pal.'

'I'm fixing up a job for Lymon. Another security van heist. This Thursday. I'll give you when and where Lymon will be intercepting the van and you can ambush him.'

Dempsey smiled knowingly. 'I'm finally beginning to figure you out,' he told the fat man. 'You're the guy who arranged Miller's last job. That's why Lymon got on your tail.'

The fat man nodded silently.

Dempsey continued, 'You been in this game awhile, haven't you?'

'Yes,' he admitted.

'You on any of our files?'

'No. I've always played it safe. Kept well behind the scenes. Always avoided trouble . . .'

'Until now.'

'Yes.'

Dempsey eyed him speculatively. 'Seems to me, Mr Mastermind, that you're quite a catch. In fact you're a bigger fish than Lymon himself . . .'

'Yes, but I'm no psychopath. You know as well as I do that Lymon, sooner or later, is going to go off like a fragmentation grenade and a lot of people are going to get hurt. He's a top priority problem for you. You need to get him fast.'

'True,' admitted Dempsey. 'But you're expecting a lot if you think we can just let you walk away scot-free with *your* track record.'

After a pause the fat man said, 'I'll throw in something else as part of the deal.'

'Such as?'

'I'll promise to retire. No more jobs. Time I quit anyway. Getting too old for this sort of stress. What do you say?'

'It's a possibility but I can't make any promises until I talk to my chief,' Dempsey told him.

'I understand.'

'But there's one thing *I* don't understand,' said Dempsey.

'What is it?'

'You know where Lymon's holed up right now, don't you?'

A shadow passed across the fat man's face. 'Yes.'

'Then why don't you just tell me the address and we'll move in on him today. No need to wait until Thursday.'

'No!' said the fat man unexpectedly loudly. 'That's out of the question. There are . . . there are reasons. Good ones. I can't explain right now.'

'Okay, okay, take it easy,' said Dempsey. 'Thursday it is . . .'

Sitting on a park bench far away, Makepeace was wishing she could lip-read as she peered through her powerful binoculars at Dempsey and the fat man. She felt guilty at disobeying Dempsey's orders in this fashion but had made up her mind that she was doing the right thing.

She made a slow, sweeping pan with the binoculars — something she'd been doing periodically since arriving at her chosen position — pausing only to zero in on individuals or couples to ensure there was nothing suspicious about them. Then, in the woods that screened the Ladies Bathing Pond, she spotted the figure of a man moving among the trees. '*Men*,' she muttered disgustedly to herself, remembering a friend who used the pool regularly telling her that men often lurked in the wood in order to spy on the women bathers, many of whom went topless . . .

Then Makepeace realized that it was far too cold for any one to be using the pool today, unless they were health-nuts of the most eccentric kind. She focussed in on the man and saw that he was not looking in the direction of the Bathing Pond but in the direction of the Highgate Ponds. And he too was holding up a pair of binoculars to his eyes.

As her heartbeat began to quicken she studied him carefully. She couldn't see his face clearly because of his binoculars but he appeared to be in his mid-thirties, was fair-skinned and had very short blond hair. He was wearing a dark green jacket with a hood attached and brown cord trousers.

Makepeace frowned. She was in a dilemma. She couldn't see any sign of a weapon but she felt fairly certain that the man in the woods was the same one that Dempsey and she had encountered the night before last. He was certainly the right height and build. But what should she do? Try and sneak up on him from behind? But that would take ages and if his intention was to kill Dempsey he would have done so long before she got close enough to him to use her .32.

No, the first priority was to warn Dempsey . . .

She got up from the bench and began to walk towards the Pond — quickly, but not fast enough to attract unwanted attention. She had forced her long blonde hair into an uncomfortable woollen cap so she hoped she could get within earshot of Dempsey without the man in the woods recognizing her. As an extra precaution she slipped on her dark glasses . . .

As she walked she kept her eyes fixed on the distant figure, pausing occasionally for a quick look through the binoculars. If she saw any sign of a weapon she would have no choice but to fire her own gun into the air to alert Dempsey. But she hoped she wouldn't have to do that.

She was about eighty yards from the fat man and Dempsey when she saw the figure in the woods start to move forward. She slowed her walk and raised the binoculars. Her stomach gave an unpleasant heave when she saw a metallic glint as he took something from a case she hadn't noticed before . . .

She let the binoculars drop on their strap and started to run. 'Dempsey!' she yelled. 'Dempsey!'

Dempsey was arranging with the fat man the time and place of their next meeting when he heard his name being called. He turned and saw a woman running towards him across the Heath. He knew immediately it was Makepeace. 'Damn!' he cried.

The fat man had turned too. 'You lied to me!' he cried accusingly. 'You said you came alone! Well, that's that — the deal's off. I'm going . . .'

But by then Dempsey had seen that Makepeace was frantically pointing at something as she ran. He looked in the direction she was pointing — and saw a man moving among some trees. He was carrying something long and shiny . . .

The Bogeyman! Or Lymon . . .?

Dempsey dived behind a nearby wooden seat. 'Looks like you were lying too,' he snarled at the fat man as he drew his Colt Cobra.

The fat man stared at him in confusion. 'What . . .?'

'Your friend . . . in those trees over there,' Dempsey told him, indicating the spot with his gun. 'You set me up for Lymon. Or someone . . .'

At the mention of Lymon's name the colour drained from the fat man's face. 'Lymon *here*?! Oh no!' He turned and peered anxiously towards the woods. 'He'll kill me for sure now!'

Makepeace arrived, panting, and took cover beside Dempsey. 'You see him?'

'Yeah, but why hasn't he fired yet?'

The figure had stopped moving now and was hiding behind a tree. He was well outside the range of both Dempsey's and Makepeace's handguns but they were well aware they were in his rifle range . . .

'What *is* he doing?' Makepeace asked as the fat man, after dithering back and forth, suddenly launched himself into the pond sending the ducks scattering with angry squawks.

'I don't know but it's a real class act.'

'Aren't you going to say thanks?'

'Thanks. I'll chew your ass out later for disobeying me.'

'Dempsey, the day your teeth and my *ass* are even in close proximity will be the day . . .'

'Hey look! The guy's pullin' back!'

She saw it was true. The man was retreating into the woods. Dempsey emerged from behind the bench. 'I'm goin' after him,' he said as he began to move, crouching low, towards the trees. 'Keep an eye on the human Hippo. Don't let him get away!'

'Dempsey!' she cried 'He's got a rifle! He'll pick you off before you can get near him. You don't stand a chance!'

But he ignored her.

Chapter TEN

The killer was furious. The bitch had taken him completely by surprise. She had no right to be there. He had heard, via his bug, Dempsey order her to stay away . . .

As he ran he put the directional mike back in its case. He had been so involved in getting close enough to Dempsey and the fat man to hear what they were saying that he hadn't noticed the approach of Dempsey's partner until it was too late.

He passed through the woods like a jungle animal, making as little noise as possible. In his mind's eye he visualized the quickest route to where his car was parked in Hampstead Road. He had spent an hour studying a map of the Heath earlier that day and every detail was fresh. He made it a point to always familiarize himself, down to the smallest detail, with the areas in which he would be operating so that he would have alternative avenues of escape to choose from if anything went wrong. It was one of his many professional qualities that he took a special pride in.

He decided to take a path that would lead up around the Kenwood House Gallery and into the North Woods. Then it would only be a short distance to his car . . .

He glanced over his shoulder. No sign of pursuit. He entered Ken Wood and found the required path. No longer hindered by shrubs and other undergrowth between the trees he put on speed. He also started to relax. He was out of danger now . . .

He turned a curve in the path and came to a dead halt. Ahead of him, less than ten feet away, was Dempsey — his Colt Cobra pointing straight at him.

'Hi pal,' said Dempsey. 'Surprised to see me? I took a short cut. I figured you'd . . .'

The killer flung his black case at Dempsey. It struck his arm, knocking his gun aside. The killer had launched himself at Dempsey while the case was still in the air. Before Dempsey had time to react he was on him. He dug his stiffened fingers into a pressure point in the centre of Dempsey's upper stomach. It had the desired effect. Dempsey went momentarily limp. Then the killer chopped with the edge of his hand against another pressure point — this one being on the inside of Dempsey's right elbow. Dempsey groaned and his Colt dropped from paralysed fingers . . .

Another vicious chop, this time at the same point in Dempsey's neck where he'd hit him before, and the killer had the satisfaction of seeing him topple backwards.

Dempsey lay there, semi-conscious and groaning. The killer stood over him, feeling totally frustrated.

Dempsey was helpless — he could so easily kill him now but he mustn't. There was no Lymon or anyone else around that the blame could be pinned on — just him . . .

He cursed to himself. Why did this job have to be so damn complicated? Why couldn't it be a simple, clear-cut hit . . .?

The next thing he knew he was falling backwards. Even before he hit the ground he realized that Dempsey had used an old Judo trick on him — hooking one foot behind his heel and pushing just below his knee with the sole of his other foot. He had underestimated Dempsey — *again.*

The impact of the fall sent a searingly hot pain through his side and he knew he'd opened up the wound in his side. He twisted his body desperately. He knew what Dempsey would be doing now . . .

A glance showed him that he was right. Dempsey's fingers were already closing on the butt of the dropped Colt Cobra. The killer sprang up like a cat and leapt for cover. Behind him the Colt boomed. The bullet passed so close to his head he heard the *zinging* sound it made as it just missed his ear. But then he had the cover of the trees between him and Dempsey, and knew he was safe. He doubted if Dempsey was in any shape to pursue him any distance . . .

When Dempsey returned to the Pond he saw that the fat man was sitting huddled on the bench, shivering from the cold. He had Makepeace's jacket draped around his shoulders.

Makepeace regarded Dempsey with concern as he slumped down on the bench beside the fat man. 'Are you all right?' she asked worriedly.

'No,' he growled. His neck throbbed painfully and he felt dizzy.

'What happened?'

'I almost had him. I even had the *drop* on the guy,' said Dempsey, his voice heavy with self-disgust. 'Then he threw this at me ...' He lifted up the black case. 'And the roof fell in on me. Then he got away.' Dempsey turned to the fat man. 'You still claim that guy isn't one of your boys?'

'Yes!' he cried, his jowls quivering from the cold. 'I don't know who he is — unless he's a mate of Lymon's.'

Makepeace took the case from Dempsey and opened it. She frowned when she saw the directional mike and earphones. 'What happened to the rifle?' she asked, taking the mike out of the case.

Dempsey frowned too. 'I don't know. He wasn't carrying it when I jumped him. I just guessed it was in that case ...'

She put the earphones on, switched the mike on and pointed its long pick-up rod in the direction of a distant couple walking with their Labrador dog on the Heath. She listened intently.

After several moments Makepeace said, 'How very interesting. His name is Roy. Her name is June, and they're worried about someone called Robert finding out about their relationship. The dog's name, by the way is Ronnie ...' She took the earphones off. 'Quite a gadget.'

'So it wasn't a rifle we spotted, it was that,' said Dempsey, puzzled. 'He was eavesdropping on us ...'

'Maybe it wasn't the same one who tried to kill you before,' said Makepeace.

'It was him all right. Guy's got to be a karate black belt. Even hit me in the same place on my neck. But he didn't try to kill me. He had a chance — he could have done it easy, but he didn't. Why?'

Makepeace couldn't answer him.

The fat man was still shivering. 'At least it proves he wasn't with me. If he was he wouldn't have to eavesdrop on me, would he?'

'He's got a point,' said Makepeace.

'Yeah,' sighed Dempsey. 'So who the hell *is* he with?'

'Did you get a good look at him this time?'

Dempsey nodded. 'Never seen him before. When we get back to headquarters I'll put together a computer-generated indentikit picture of his face and see what the files throw up. If anything . . .' He turned to the shivering fat man. 'You'd better get into some dry clothes pretty quick. Can we give you a ride anywhere. Or maybe call you a cab?'

'I wasn't born yesterday, Lieutenant. You two go. I'll stay here until I'm sure you've gone. Don't try to follow me. You just get that deal we talked of approved by your superiors.'

'I'll do my best,' Dempsey assured him.

'I'll call you this time tomorrow. If the deal is a go-ahead I'll give you the details of the job.'

'Right,' said Dempsey. He got slowly to his feet. 'Come on Makepeace, let's go . . .'

As they walked across the Heath Makepeace looked at Dempsey and said with concern, 'Are you feeling ill? You're as white as a sheet.'

'A bit dizzy, that's all.'

'I'll take you back to headquarters in my car,' she told him firmly. 'You can't drive if you're dizzy.'

To her surprise he didn't protest. He *must* be feeling ill, she thought worriedly. 'What's the deal you've worked out with our fat friend?' she asked.

Dempsey told her. She said, 'You think Spikings will agree to it?'

'He'd better,' said Dempsey grimly.

They walked the rest of the way to her car in silence.

It wasn't until they'd got into the car that Dempsey spoke again. 'Princess, the guy treated me like a rag doll — like I was nothing. I got to face the truth, I've lost my edge for sure. I'm out of the game . . .'

'Dempsey, don't talk nonsense. You said yourself he was probably a black belt . . . Dempsey?'

He had suddenly slumped against her. Her initial thought that he was trying something on was quickly discarded as she realized he was unconscious.

She pushed him back into his seat and undid his collar and tie. Then she felt for his pulse.

She couldn't find it.

Lymon was waiting when Rose returned to his St John's Wood house.

'Where you been?' Lymon asked him suspiciously as he entered the front hallway.

'Doing business,' Rose informed him curtly. 'Don't worry. It doesn't concern you.'

'It better not,' said Lymon then wrinkled his nose as Rose hung up his overcoat. 'Bloody hell, you stink! What happened to you?'

'Had a little accident.'

'Smells like a big one to me,' said Lymon and laughed.

After he'd had a bath and changed, Rose went back downstairs and showed Lymon a map of the area where the job was to take place.

'The security company delivers the factory wages

every Thursday at 10 a.m. regular as clockwork,' explained Rose. 'Now naturally they vary the route the van takes each week, which is standard security procedure, but they can only vary the route up to this point of the journey . . .' He pointed at the spot on the map.

'You see, it's a chemical factory and has been built in the middle of nowhere for reasons of safety. See, there are no houses around for miles. The factory is only accessible via the one road which was built especially for it. Greenfield Road. See?'

Lymon nodded.

'So you got to get your truck to this turning well before 10 a.m. so that you can get to these woods here about a mile from the factory. You hide the truck in the woods and when the van comes you . . .'

'I know what to do,' said Lymon impatiently.

'I'm sure you do. Anyway your escape car had better not be late. And you're going to need a good driver because if you don't get all the way back up Greenfield Road to the main road after the alarm's been raised the police will be able to block it off . . .'

'Don't worry. No one's gonna be raisin' any bleedin' alarm,' said Lymon coldly.

Rose shook his head, 'You don't understand. No matter how fast you take care of the driver and crew you won't be able to stop an alarm going off. It's an automatic one, built into the vans. Soon as you blow it open a signal is transmitted to the company's head office. It also pinpoints the van's exact position. The security people get on the blower to the cops and, well, you get the picture.'

Lymon gave him a dirty look. 'Yeah.'

'So that's why I said you need a good driver. Now I can recommend a really ace one. He's been doing jobs for me for years but never once been . . .'

Lymon was shaking his head. 'I'll pick me own driver.'

'Oh. Okay. Got one in mind?'

'Yeah.'

'Who is he? I'll tell you if he's good.'

'No. The less you know, the better I'll feel. Know what I mean?'

Rose nodded. He'd got the message.

After a long, uncomfortable pause he said, 'Uh, what are your plans afterwards? After the job, I mean?'

A sly expression crept into Lymon's eyes. 'Thought I might take your advice after all.'

'*My* advice?'

'Yeah. 'Bout Spain. Remember? You said you had contacts over there.'

'Oh, yes, *yes.* Fine! I'll get in touch with them today. Tell them to expect you.'

'Yeah. You do that,' said Lymon and lit a cigarette. Rose noticed that there was a half-smile on his face, as if he was amused at some private joke. Rose had a horrible idea that the joke was going to be on him . . .

Dempsey was running down a long, black corridor. At the far end was an open doorway with light streaming through it. He knew that as soon as he went through the doorway he would be safe. But no matter how fast he ran he couldn't seem to get any closer to the doorway . . .

He looked down. He was wearing jeans and sneakers. He remembered those sneakers. They'd been a present from his aunt on his ninth birthday.

Then he realized how small his legs looked. He

looked at his arms. A child's arms . . .

He heard the footsteps behind him. He looked over his shoulder. A tall man dressed entirely in black was running after him along the corridor. The only part of his face that was visible were his eyes. They glowed red.

It was *the Bogeyman.*

Dempsey increased his efforts to reach the doorway but now it was receding into the distance. The faster he ran the further away it got.

While behind him the footsteps of his pursuer grew louder.

Then he felt a hand on his shoulder . . .

'Mr Dempsey! Mr Dempsey!'

He tried to shake off the hand gripping his shoulder but he couldn't. 'No, no . . .' he groaned. 'Let me go . . .'

'Mr Dempsey! Wake up!'

He opened his eyes. A face swam into focus. A girl's face. A pretty girl's face. She had curly black hair and a nurse's cap. He tried to sit up but she gently restrained him.

'Calm down, Mr Dempsey, you're all right. Relax.'

He tried to look around to see where he was but his movements were restricted by something encasing his neck. He put his hand up and discovered he was wearing a thick, sponge-rubber collar.

'What the hell is this?' he demanded angrily. 'And where the hell am I?'

'It's a surgical collar,' said the girl. 'And you're in the Middlesex Hospital.'

'Hospital? That's crazy. I'm fine! Listen Sister, I got to get out of here. I got things to do!'

'Firstly, I'm not a Sister. I'm just a junior nurse. And secondly, you're not going anywhere until your doctor says you can. So just calm down and relax. You're a sick man.'

'*Sick*! I'm not sick, Nurse . . . Nurse whatever-your-name-is . . .'

'Headlong.'

'What?'

'Headlong. That's my name. Holly Headlong.'

Dempsey, momentarily distracted, stared at her and said, 'You're kiddin'!'

'No, that's my name okay. You can check it in the phone book if you don't believe me.'

He grinned at her. 'The phone book? Hey, is that an invitation?'

A slight flush appeared on both her cheeks, making her even more attractive. 'Certainly not! I've only just met you.'

Dempsey raised himself against his pillows to get a better look at her. He saw she had an impressive figure and her legs, encased in their black stockings, were long. 'So?' he said.

'So I think you're one of those people who entertain a popular misconception about nurses,' she told him sternly. 'Namely that we are sex-mad and will hop into bed with every man that comes along.'

'Hey!' he said, sounding aggrieved. 'You got me wrong. I don't think that at all. And I've known a lot of nurses in my time, believe me. Look, you said we've only just met — true — but I was attracted to you the first moment I saw you. What's wrong with you admitting that you're attracted to me too?'

She gazed at him in amazement. 'Has anyone ever told you you're incredibly egotistical?'

He grinned. 'All the time.'

'Well, I'm not sur . . .' She stopped when the door suddenly opened. A tall man in his early forties entered the room. He gave Dempsey a beaming smile, ignoring Nurse Headlong.

'Back among the living, are we, Lieutenant? Good, good . . .' He spoke with an upper class accent and Dempsey instantly disliked him. *Patronizing creep*, he thought. *He must be a doctor.*

'I'm Doctor Masefield,' he said as he pulled a chair over to the side of Dempsey's bed and sat down. 'How are we feeling?'

'I don't know about you, Doc, but I'm feeling fine. When do I get out of this place?'

Doctor Masefield laughed, making it seem as if Dempsey had just said the funniest thing in weeks but at the same time making the laughter sound condescending. Dempsey's dislike for him increased.

'My dear fellow, I'm afraid you will be our guest for at least a week . . .'

'A week!' cried Dempsey. 'No way! Out of the question! I can't stay here for a week! I got an important job to wrap up!'

'My dear Lieutenant Dempsey, you have no choice in the matter,' said the doctor in the manner of a kindly but firm uncle addressing a wayward child. 'You have sustained a potentially serious injury to your neck. Not only do you have a fractured vertebra but the massive internal bruising is putting pressure on your carotid artery and restricting the flow of blood to your brain. Which is why you lost consciousness earlier. You must have absolute rest for the next few days to allow the internal swelling to subside.'

'Let me get this straight, Doc. You're telling me if I don't take things easy I'm gonna drop dead?'

The doctor pursed his lips, obviously regarding the mention of death in his presence as a medical *faux pas*. Then he said, 'It's a possibility. You certainly run the risk of losing consciousness again.'

'I see,' said Dempsey sombrely.

'Good,' said the doctor with a beaming smile. He patted Dempsey's hand as if rewarding a dog for doing a difficult trick.

Dempsey said, 'Now, Doc, will you go fetch my clothes. I'm getting *out* of here.'

Chapter
ELEVEN

'You have a visitor,' announced Nurse Headlong. 'But she can only stay a short time.' She then ushered in Makepeace and, after giving her a vaguely resentful look, closed the door.

'Nice looking girl,' commented Makepeace as she came over to the bed.

'Yeah. Name's Holly Headlong. Take a seat.'

'Holly Headlong? You're joking,' said Makepeace as she sat down.

'That's what I thought but I checked her name tag on her uniform. It's true.'

'So how are you feeling?'

'I *feel* okay but according to the medic I got a problem with the blood getting to my brain.'

'I've been telling you that for ages,' she said with a smile.

He scowled at her.

'Sorry. Actually you gave me a real scare. For a few moments I thought you were dead. I couldn't find your pulse.'

'I can't remember flaking out. What happened?'

'We'd just got in the car. Suddenly you just collapsed on top of me.'

'I *did*?' He raised his eyebrows then said regretfully, 'Damn, the experience of a lifetime and I'm unconscious during it.'

Ignoring the comment, Makepeace continued, 'When I found out you weren't dead I rushed you straight here. And the rest you know.'

Dempsey fingered his surgical collar. 'Yeah. And the medic says I'm gonna be stuck here for at least a week. I tried to walk out of here but no dice. Wouldn't give me my clothes back.'

'Of course not. Dempsey, I've spoken to your doctor. He explained the situation. You've *got* to stay here. So why not relax and enjoy yourself. You need the rest anyway. And this place seems pretty comfortable . . .' She glanced around. 'Even a colour TV. I hope we didn't offend your socialist principles by fixing you up with a private room.'

'*What* socialist principles?' growled Dempsey. 'You know I'm no commie!'

'A joke, Dempsey. Just a joke.'

'Look, princess, I *can't* stay here for a week. There's the heist on Thursday. I gotta arrange the deal with the fat man. And I want to be there when we nab Lymon. No way am I gonna miss that!'

Makepeace sighed. 'I talked to Spikings about it. He's not happy. Said it sounded too risky . . .'

'God*damn*!' bellowed Dempsey, thumping the side of the bed with his fist.

'Now calm down . . .'

'See! I'm out of the way for just a few hours and everything goes down the tubes. You guys *need* me . . .!'

'Dempsey, you are *not* indispensable. We managed at S.I.10 before you arrived and we shall no doubt manage perfectly well after you go back to America.'

'Crap. You know your success rate at S.I.10 has gone up by ten percent since I joined the shop.'

'Just a coincidence,' she told him airily. 'Besides, your success rate hasn't been too good recently, has it?'

He looked pained. 'You don't have to rub it in, princess.'

'I'm sorry. I didn't mean . . .'

Just then the door opened and Nurse Headlong reappeared. 'I'm sorry, Sergeant Makepeace, but I must ask you to leave. Lieutenant Dempsey needs to rest.'

Makepeace smiled and shrugged. 'All right, I'll go quietly, officer.' As she rose from the chair Dempsey said urgently, 'I gotta speak to Spikings. Soon as possible. Got to make him see sense on this Lymon set-up. Fix it, will ya?'

'I'll do what I can,' she promised. 'In the meantime do what this nurse says and rest.'

On the way out she said to Nurse Headlong, 'You will take *good* care of him, won't you?'

'Of course,' answered Nurse Headlong, a little huffily.

Makepeace gave Dempsey a quick wink over her shoulder as she left.

When the door had closed Nurse Headlong cleared her throat and said, 'She's very pretty.'

Dempsey, his mind on other things, said, 'Who?'

'The lady who just left.'

'What? Oh, Makepeace. Yeah, I guess she is.'

'Is she your girlfriend?'

'Makepeace?!' Dempsey gave a laugh. 'Hell no. We just work together.'

'You see a lot of her?'

'Yeah.' But not as much of her as I'd like to see, he said to himself. 'She's my partner.'

'You talk together as if you were married.'

He was genuinely shocked by this observation. 'Yeah? Hell! That's scary!'

'You don't fancy her then?'

'Makepeace? Nah, no way,' he lied.

After a pause, she said, 'Do you have a girlfriend?'

'No. Not at the moment.'

For the first time since Makepeace's visit Nurse Headlong smiled.

Harry Rose lay in bed next to Beth. He couldn't sleep. It had been a bad night. Dinner, like breakfast, had been an ordeal but in a different way. This time Beth had been meticulously polite to Lymon, putting on an exaggerated display of hospitality that was so obviously a sham that he had been a nervous wreck by the time the meal was over. He could see that Lymon knew he was being got at and expected him at any moment to erupt.

When he'd got Beth alone in the kitchen later and told her to stop it she'd replied coldly that she was merely following his instructions to the letter.

The rest of the evening was no better. Lymon had slouched in front of the TV watching videos all night, depriving Beth of her favourite soaps. The atmosphere in the living room had been so poisonous that a whiff of cyanide would have acted as an air freshener.

It was going to be like this until Thursday. And then

what . . . ? He didn't believe Lymon's story about Spain. No, Lymon planned to kill him after the job, he was sure of that. Maybe he intended to hide out in this very house, terrorizing Beth into obeying his wishes, or perhaps he intended to kill her too.

His only chance was Dempsey. Dempsey *had* to get his superiors to accept the deal. And then he had to get Lymon.

He sighed, turned and tentatively reached to touch Beth's shoulder. 'Beth, are you awake?' he asked quietly.

'Don't touch me,' she hissed. 'Don't ever touch me again!'

Spikings arrived early the following morning, and in a foul mood. If Dempsey had been expecting Spikings to display even a token amount of sympathy for his condition he was immediately disappointed. On the contrary, Spikings gave the impression he held Dempsey entirely responsible for his ending up in hospital.

But Dempsey did manage to persuade Spikings to agree to the fat man's deal. He even got Spikings to use his influence to have a phone installed in the room. When the fat man made his call that afternoon the S.I.10 operator would patch him through to the hospital.

By the time Spikings left, Dempsey felt that he had at least achieved *something*, though he was still far from happy at having to remain in hospital. And things weren't improved by the fact that his day nurse was a complete contrast to Holly Headlong. Called Nurse Mitchell, she was a large, middle-aged Irish woman with the disposition of a police dog and a face to match.

His spirits were raised slightly at lunchtime when Makepeace paid him another visit. She entered carrying a large, brown paper bag. 'A present,' she said, handing it to him,

He examined its contents. 'Oranges, apples, bananas ... I don't see any half pint of bourbon stashed in here.'

'That's because there *isn't* a half pint of bourbon stashed in there.'

'Hey, princess, what's the point of giving me a bag of fruit then?' he complained.

'The point is the fruit itself. You are supposed to eat it. It's *good* for you.'

He gave her a pained looked and handed the bag back to her. '*You* eat it. I need a drink. I'm goin' stir crazy in this place. I'll be climbing the walls if I have to spend a week here.'

Makepeace took an apple from the bag and began to eat it. Between mouthfuls she said, 'I hear congratulations are in order. You talked Spikings round to your way of thinking. Headquarters is already a hive of activity as we prepare for Thursday's little operation.'

'I've still got to settle the deal with the fat man,' said Dempsey sourly. 'Without me you guys are nowhere. You won't know when or where Lymon's gonna hit.'

She took a delicate bite out of her apple and said, 'Still trying to prove you're indispensable, Dempsey?'

He glowered at her and then said reluctantly, 'Who's going to lead the team?'

'Spikings himself.'

Dempsey grimaced. 'It's not right! *I* should be the one in at the finish with Lymon. It's *my* operation and I'm gonna be stuck here in bed!'

She smiled sweetly at him. 'Don't worry. I'll be

doing a video tape of the whole thing. You can watch it all on TV later in perfect comfort.'

Dempsey looked at her. 'I've changed my mind. Give me an apple.'

'You want to eat an apple?' she asked suspiciously.

'No. I wanna *throw* it at you!'

Harry Rose rang S.I.10 at the arranged time but when he asked for Dempsey he was told by the operator there would be a delay in putting him through. By the time Dempsey did come on the line Rose was suspicious.

'What's going on? What's with all the clicks and buzzing? If you're trying to trace this call you're wasting your time. I'm ringing from a call box and my car's parked just outside . . .'

'Take it easy, pal. You're not being traced. They had to transfer you to where I'm staying at the moment.'

'Yeah, and where's that?' asked Rose, still suspicious.

'Ah . . . hospital,' admitted Dempsey.

'What?'

'It's no big deal. A minor injury I got during that fight with that guy on the Heath yesterday. I'll be out in a week.'

'A week!' exclaimed Rose. 'But the job's on Thursday! You've *got* to be there. If Lymon gets away I'm . . . I'm finished.'

'Hey, cool down. The operation will go as planned without me. I'm not . . .' Dempsey paused then continued, '. . . I'm not indispensable, you know. I'm just a team member. The guys will get Lymon okay. You got no worries on that score, I promise you.'

'Well . . .' said Rose doubtfully.

'Look, the chief has agreed to your deal. You give us Lymon and keep to your promise to retire and you can just walk away scot-free. Of course, we ever get wind you're still in business, the deal's off. We grab you and put you away for keeps.'

'I'll keep my side of the bargain, don't worry,' said Rose.

'Then give me the details of Thursday's job . . . now.'

After hesitating a long time Rose told Dempsey everything about the planned heist. When he rang off, Dempsey called Makepeace. 'You get all that?'

'Every word. There isn't a dry eye in the house. We all liked the bit about you not being indispensable to S.I.10. Very touching.'

'Very funny,' growled Dempsey. 'Look, I want a map of that location right away so I can figure out a plan of action.'

'Uh-uh,' she told him. 'You're in hospital to rest. Leave Thursday to us.'

'Makepeace, don't give me that crap! This is still my pigeon!'

'Not according to Spikings,' said Makepeace. 'Sorry.'

'*Makepeace . . . !!*' he thundered but she'd already hung up.

Dempsey had calmed down somewhat by the time Holly Headlong came on duty that evening. 'You're a sight for sore eyes,' he told her with feeling. 'I couldn't have taken much more of that Irish battlewagon.'

'Nurse Mitchell? Yes, she is a bit of a dragon. A lot of the younger nurses are scared of her.' She came to the side of the bed, obviously just as pleased to see him as he was to see her. 'How are you feeling?'

'Fine and dandy. But I'd feel a hell of a lot finer if I could get this damn collar off and get out of here.'

'No chance. You're my prisoner.'

He grinned at her. 'I got no complaints about my jailer, it's the jail itself I can't stand.'

She noticed the bag of fruit on the bedside table. 'You've had a visitor,' she said, peering into it.

'Yeah. Makepeace. According to her, fruit is the answer to all my problems.'

'The bag is full. Haven't you eaten any of it?'

'Nah. I don't like fruit.'

'It's good for you.'

'Not you too. You sound like Makepeace.'

Headlong put her hand in the bag and pulled out an apple. She offered it to him. 'Go on. Eat it. For me.'

He gave her a quizzical smile. 'You trying to tempt me?'

Two small spots of red appeared high up on her cheeks. 'I might be,' she said.

'Well, if you are, the answer is yes.' He accepted the apple from her and took a large bite out of it. As he chewed he pointed at the bunch of keys hanging from her belt. 'The key to this door among them?'

'Yes. Why?'

'I was thinking you could go lock the door and then we could get to know each other better.' He patted the bed beside him in a meaningful manner.

She pretended to look shocked but he could see she wasn't really. 'Lieutenant Dempsey! Are you out of your mind!'

'Yeah, yeah, you're going to tell me you aren't a sex-mad nurse who leaps into bed with every man she meets.'

'Right!'

'But I'm an exception, right?'

'Well . . . yes,' she admitted.

'So go lock the door.'

She shook her head. 'It's out of the question. I'm on *duty.* I've got other patients to look after apart from you.'

He shrugged. 'Well, that's that then.'

'Well, it doesn't have to be,' she said slowly. The two spots of red on her cheeks were larger now.

'What do you mean?'

'I get off duty at twelve tonight. My friend Julie comes on then. I could ask her to make sure we wouldn't be disturbed.'

'Sounds fine with me.' *We have lift-off,* he thought triumphantly.

She leaned over the bed, put her arms around him and kissed him on the lips. He could feel the beat of her heart against his chest. It was beating very fast. *Maybe I've got the wrong idea about hospitals,* he told himself.

Outside the Middlesex Hospital, in Cleveland Street, a blue Ford Escort pulled to a halt. The killer stared thoughtfully at the hospital then settled back in his seat to wait.

Chapter TWELVE

The door of Dempsey's room opened dead on midnight. He waited for Holly to turn the light on but she didn't. The door closed and he heard soft footsteps as she approached his bed. Then silence.

'I didn't figure you for the shy type,' said Dempsey.

After a pause she said softly, 'Well, I am. And I'm having second thoughts about this.'

'Ignore them and go back to your first thoughts. They were much better.'

'Seriously. I'm worried about you. Doctor Masefield said you had to avoid exerting yourself.'

'So I'll take it easy. I'll leave all the hard work to you. Besides, if I get into difficulty at least there will be a trained nurse close by. *Very* close by.'

She didn't say anything.

'Hey, come on and make up your mind,' he complained. 'Otherwise the damn *suspense* will kill me!'

'Well . . .' she said slowly. Then he heard the rustle of clothing.

The killer made his move just after 1 a.m. Wearing a white lab coat with a stethescope protruding from the top pocket he strode purposefully through the hospital corridors towards Dempsey's room. The lack of security in British hospitals not only surprised him but offended his sense of professionalism. In any American hospital he would have encountered armed security guards by now.

It took him a while to locate Dempsey's room — it was a big hospital and he could hardly stop and ask for directions but finally, at 1.15, he arrived at the right room number.

His plan was simple. From the bug he had in the S.I.10 office he knew the details of Dempsey's medical condition. A pillow held down over his face would do the job. It would be presumed he died in his sleep . . .

He paused at the door and listened. At that moment a nurse came along the corridor. He gave her a polite smile and a nod as she passed. She smiled back in a preoccupied way but didn't say anything.

He opened the door, stepped into Dempsey's room, and quickly closed the door behind him. He stood there for a few moments, waiting for his eyes to adjust to the darkness and to get his bearings. He could hear the sound of breathing not far away. Dempsey was obviously in a deep sleep.

The killer moved silently towards the bed which he could now dimly perceive as a vague outline in the darkness. He reached the side of the bed and stared down. Then he frowned. Something wasn't right. The shape in the bed was confusing. Either his eyes were playing tricks on him or Dempsey had two heads . . .

He had no choice but to use the small pen torch he had in his pocket. He took it out and switched it on . . .

. . . And found himself staring into a pair of startled eyes.

But they weren't Dempsey's. They belonged to a girl. Dempsey lay asleep beside her.

The killer's mind reeled. It was the last thing he had expected. He was prepared for any number of scenarios that would require a swift adjustment of his plans, but *this* . . . in a *hospital*!

'Look, doctor, I can explain,' the girl said nervously. 'It's not what you think . . . I mean, I know it *looks* bad but you see the patient . . . well, he's . . . er . . .'

The killer backed slowly away from the bed. He couldn't kill Dempsey with her in the room. And if he killed her too he might as well leave a calling card.

'Er . . . the patient . . . the patient and I . . .' The girl was starting to babble now. 'Well, we're old friends . . . *very* old friends . . . and well, you could have knocked me over with a feather when I walked in here and saw him . . . and . . .'

The killer didn't wait to listen to anymore. He turned and fled.

'James! James! Wake up!' cried Holly urgently in his ear as she shook his shoulder.

'Whassa matter?' he mumbled sleepily. 'What's up?'

'We're in big trouble! Or rather *I* am! A doctor came in and saw us together!'

'What?' said Dempsey, coming awake now. 'What are you talking about?'

'It happened just a few moments ago. I woke up and there he was, standing beside the bed! I'm going to lose my job because of this, I know it!'

Dempsey struggled into a sitting position and put an arm around her shoulders. 'Hey, let's not hit the panic button just yet, okay? Tell me what he said . . .'

'He didn't say anything. Oh, *why* did I let you talk me into this? All those years of training down the drain . . .'

'He didn't say anything? Not a word?' said Dempsey. 'He didn't even ask you what you were doing in my bed?'

'No. He just backed away then ran out the door. I expect he's gone to report me to the Head Matron. I'd better get dressed . . .'

'Hang on,' he said, stopping her from getting out of the bed. 'Did you recognize him?'

She paused. 'I only got a quick look at him as he went out into the corridor but . . . no . . . come to think of it, I don't think I've ever seen him here before.'

'So what makes you think he was a doctor?'

'He *looked* like a doctor! I mean, he was wearing a white coat . . .'

Dempsey sighed, then he said, 'Describe him to me.'

'I told you I only got a brief glimpse of him.'

'Try anyway.'

'Well . . . he looked to be in his thirties — in his mid-thirties — and he had very short hair. I think it was blond but I'm not sure . . .'

'You don't have to tell me any more,' said Dempsey grimly. 'I know who he is. And he's no doctor.'

'He's not?' Holly asked hopefully.

'No. He's a hired killer. A professional hit-man. And *I'm* the pigeon he's out to hit.'

'Oh, thank goodness!'

'Thanks a heap,' said Dempsey sourly. 'Nice to know who your friends are.'

'Oh, I didn't mean . . .!' she cried, embarrassed. 'What I meant was . . .'

'Don't worry. I know what you meant. What I can't figure out is why he didn't do the job while he had the chance. He could have taken care of you just like that' — Dempsey snapped his fingers — 'without waking me. Then he could have wasted me at his leisure.'

'You mean — he could have *killed* me?' asked Holly in a small voice.

'Yeah. Of course I do.'

'Oh!'

'But he didn't kill either of us. And he didn't kill me in the woods yesterday when he had the chance. Why? What's his game? A hit-man who seems to only want to make a hit when the conditions are right. But what *are* those conditions? And why do they exist?'

'I don't feel well,' said Holly.

'Good thing you're in a hospital then. Come on, get up and get dressed. We're getting out of here . . .' He threw back the covers and jumped out of the bed.

'*We're* getting out of here — what are you talking about? You can't go anywhere.'

'The hell I can't! That was the last straw. I'm not going to stay here and act the dumb sitting-duck.'

'But your neck injury — it will be dangerous for you to leave hospital.'

'It's gonna be a goddamn sight more dangerous for me if I stay in hospital, so do as I say! I want you to go fetch my clothes and stuff, *now*!'

'I can't do that!' she protested. 'If I got caught I'd be in big trouble!'

'I promise you I'll take full responsibility. I got ways of fixin' things. So get moving!'

'But you won't be able to just walk out at this time of night without someone noticing you.'

'Okay then, grab me a white coat as well.'
'A white coat?'
'So I'll look like a doctor.'
'Oh.'
'Now will you get that cute little ass of yours into gear and *move* it!'
Holly was gone nearly half an hour. When she returned Dempsey said eagerly, 'You get everything?'
'Yes, but don't think it was easy,' she said as she dropped what appeared to be a bundle of laundry on the bed. He opened the bag and saw his clothes, shoes and a white coat.
'Holly, you're marvellous,' he told her as he dressed rapidly. 'We'll leave together. A doctor and a nurse acting real friendly together. No one will give us a second look, right?'
'I guess not.'
'Good. You got a car?'
'On a nurse's salary? You must be joking.'
'Damn.' Dempsey thought for a few moments then looked at the phone. I'll call a mini-cab. Have it waiting at the front entrance.'
'Where are we going? If you don't mind me asking.'
'My place. Unless you got any objections?'
'No. I don't have any objections.' She suddenly smiled at him. 'Actually I'm beginning to find all this rather exciting.'
Dempsey rolled his eyes. *Women*! he thought, *who can figure them*?

The killer groaned inwardly when he saw that the voluble middle-aged woman was on the night desk again. And as he feared she immediately launched into a rambling interrogation when he asked for his key.

Had he been out to see a show in the West End? Was he finding it easy to find his way around London? Wasn't the weather awful and so on.

He did something he instantly regretted. 'Shut up you stupid bitch and just give me my key!' he snapped.

She stared at him in astonishment, then handed him his key without another word.

Stupid! Stupid! Stupid! he told himself as he went up to his room. He'd never acted so unprofessionally before. Never in his whole career. He was letting this job get to him. But no wonder, with all the crazy screw-ups. He still hadn't recovered from the shock of finding that girl in Dempsey's hospital bed. No way could he have anticipated *that*! No way at all. Or maybe he should have done some checking around first. Maybe it was the norm in this country. Maybe there was some crazy kind of Blue Cross scheme available here that provided you with tail in hospitals as well as medical insurance? Anything was possible in this crazy country . . .

When he got to his room he took a hot shower, put a new dressing on his chest wound — *the bitch was still bleeding* — and then did another unprofessional thing. He opened the bottle of Scotch he'd been saving to celebrate the successful culmination of the contract. Normally he never drank on the job but he justified this exception to the rule by telling himself he needed to relax and clear his mind. He had to find a solution to the problem . . .

It was getting light and the bottle was half empty when the killer finally smiled to himself. He had the solution he needed. A plan that would enable him to not only rub out Dempsey but his bitch of a partner, Makepeace, as well.

Chapter
THIRTEEN

Makepeace couldn't believe her eyes when she walked into the office the next morning and saw Dempsey at his desk.

'What on earth are you doing here?' she cried.

'What's it look like?' he said, not glancing up from the map he was studying. 'I'm working. Like you should be.'

'No. I mean what are you doing out of hospital so soon?'

'I kinda discharged myself, unofficial-like. With a little help from a nurse . . .'

'Nurse Headlong, I presume.'

Dempsey looked up from the map and grinned at her. 'Yeah. We had a long talk last night and she finally saw my point of view.'

'I'll bet she did,' said Makepeace drily.

'So here I am, ready and rarin' to go.'

'Yes, straight to the morgue, you idiot. Don't you realize you could drop dead at any moment?'

'Princess, do I *look* like I'm going to drop dead at any moment?'

'How should I know? I've never seen you drop dead — *yet*.'

'I feel fine.'

'You're not even wearing your surgical collar.'

'Had to leave it in the room. Couldn't sneak out of the hospital disguised as a doctor with that thing round my neck. Besides, it itched.'

'Dempsey, you're mad!' cried Makepeace in exasperation. 'If you don't go back to hospital you stand a good chance of *dying*! Don't you understand that?'

'I understand that if I go back to hospital I'll stand an even better chance of getting snuffed,' said Dempsey, then told her of the events of the previous night.

'Dempsey, you never cease to amaze me,' she said when he'd finished. 'You're in hospital at death's door and sex is still the thing uppermost in your mind.' She shook her head disapprovingly. 'Fancy luring an innocent young nurse into your bed ...'

'Jealous, princess?'

Makepeace reddened. 'Don't be ridiculous!'

Dempsey laughed then said, 'If I hadn't *lured* her into my bed — as you put it — I'd probably be dead by now. Holly being there caught the guy unawares. Scared him off.'

'If it *was* him. You said you didn't see him yourself.'

'It was him okay.'

'Then why didn't he simply kill the pair of you?'

Dempsey scratched his chin. 'Yeah, that's got me foxed as well, along with why he didn't kill me when he had the chance on the Heath. Yet we know for sure that the guy has made two attempts to kill me before. It just doesn't make sense.'

'Do you still think he's somehow hooked up with Lymon?'

Before Dempsey could answer her, Spikings entered the office. He did a large double-take when he saw Dempsey, then bellowed: 'What the bloody hell are you doing here?!'

Dempsey groaned. 'I've just been through all that with Makepeace, Chief. I feel okay and I'm back on the job so let's just leave it at that, huh?'

'Dempsey, I saw your medical report at the hospital!' cried Spikings. 'I don't care how you feel — according to your doctor you're a very sick man!'

Dempsey shrugged. 'Doctors. What do they know?'

'A damn sight more than you, Lieutenant, unless you've got a medical degree lurking in your background that I don't know about.'

'I tell you I feel okay.'

'And I'm telling you, Yank, — that in your condition you're a bleeding liability! You could pass out at any moment! I can't take the chance of sending you out on a job like that. You'd be a danger not only to yourself but to the rest of the team!'

Dempsey looked Spikings in the eye and said quietly, 'I'll take full responsibility. I screw up and you can have my resignation, if I'm still breathin'. But I *have* to see this Lymon operation through to the end. I'm gonna be at that spot tomorrow . . .' He pointed at the position on the map where the fat man had told him the heist would take place. '. . . either with the team or on my lonesome. You just try and keep me away.'

Spikings' already mottled complexion grew more

mottled. 'You insubordinate bastard ...' he fumed.

'Sorry Chief,' said Dempsey, without sounding the least bit apologetic. 'But that's the way the cookie crumbles. I got to have Lymon.'

It took several moments for Spikings to regain control of himself, then he said in a low, murderous voice, 'Very well, Lieutenant. As you have me over a barrel I have no choice but to let you take part in tomorrow's operation. But I warn you that if your medical condition in any way jeopardizes the operation itself or the lives of any of the S.I.10 team members I will personally see to it that you go to prison — if you're still alive, that is.'

At 2 a.m. that night Harry Rose, who knew he'd never be able to go to sleep, got out of bed and went downstairs, taking care to tip-toe past the spare room where Lymon was, hopefully, asleep.

Rose went to his study at the rear of the house, sat down at his desk and lit a cigarette. Not long to go now, he told himself fearfully, and it would all be over — one way or the other.

He opened one of the drawers in the desk, pulled out the stack of bank statements and old cheque books it contained, then lifted up the false bottom of the drawer. Beneath it lay a Smith & Wesson .38 revolver wrapped in a plastic bag. Alongside the gun were three boxes of ammunition.

Rose slowly unwrapped the gun and stared at it with a frown on his face. He didn't like guns and in fact had never fired one. But some years ago, almost on a whim, he'd acquired this one and hidden it in the desk where it had remained ever since. Its presence, however, had disturbed him. He, who always took such great pains to distance himself from his criminal colleagues and their activities, was well aware of the risk he was running by keeping a handgun in his home, but though he'd often considered getting rid of it he hadn't.

Now, as he gazed at it, he wondered what he could do with it. One possibility was to sneak into the spare room with it, put it against the sleeping Lymon's head and pull the trigger. But he knew he'd never be able to do that. He just didn't have the nerve. And the chances were that he wouldn't be able to get close enough to Lymon anyway. The young thug slept lightly and had frighteningly quick reflexes. He also slept with the shotgun beside his bed . . .

And even if he did succeed in shooting Lymon as he slept, what then? The police would come and how would he explain the body of a wanted criminal in his spare room?

No, he would have to wait and see what developed in the morning. If Lymon forced him to it he would use the gun — if he had the chance . . .

Slowly and methodically he loaded the revolver, stared at it again for a time, then put it in the pocket of his dressing gown. Then he lit another cigarette. *How did I get into this mess*, he wondered?

Five a.m. at S.I.10 headquarters. Dempsey was overseeing the final preparations for the morning's operation while Makepeace watched him with a worried expression.

'Are you sure you're feeling all right?' she asked him, after he'd finished going over the plan of action with the others.

'Princess, that's the fifth time you've asked me that

stupid question in the last half hour,' he said irritably. 'And the answer's still the same — I feel great.'

She didn't believe him. His face had a waxy pallor to it and there were dark circles under his eyes.

'You got your video gear ready?' he asked her.

'I'm not handling the video today. Dave is.'

Dempsey frowned. 'Oh yeah. Who says so?'

'Spikings.'

His frown deepened. 'Let me take a wild guess and say the Chief told you to nurse-maid me, right?'

'My lips are sealed.'

'Hah! That'll be the day.' Dempsey went over to Dave Barnes. 'You got the video I hear.'

'Yeah.'

'My good side, huh?'

Dave grinned. 'You got it, boss.'

Makepeace said, 'He means he wants you to just shoot the back of his head.'

'Princess, any more wisecracks and I'm not going to invite you to my funeral,' Dempsey told her.

'I don't think that's funny,' she said seriously.

'Same as your wisecracks.'

Chas gave a brief knock on Spikings' door and went in.

'Yeah?' said Spikings. He was cleaning his revolver.

'I think we should call it off, guv,' said Chas.

'What do you mean?'

'Phone the security company; cancel the delivery.'

'I do that, Dempsey'll go off after Lymon on his own.'

'Dempsey. That's the nub of the problem, guv. I just don't see why we should risk a blood-bath confrontaton so he can make amends for the previous fiascos . . .'

Spikings narrowed his eyes. 'Is this an unofficial deputation? Are you speaking for the boys?'

'They'll give you everything. You know that, but they're worried about Dempsey . . .'

'*They're* worried!' said Spikings with feeling.

'I mean, with him in his condition . . .'

'You don't have to tell me but you know the situation. My hands are tied. We have to go through with it . . .'

At that moment the door opened and Dempsey stuck his head round it. 'Hey, it's party time. You guys coming or what?'

Spikings glanced at Chas and said, 'Yeah, we're coming.'

Harry Rose had been wrong. He *did* eventually fall asleep. But not for long. Something hard prodded him in the side of his face, waking him up.

He opened his eyes to find himself staring into the double barrels of Lymon's shotgun.

'Wakey-wakey, Harry,' said Lymon quietly.

Oh no! thought Rose. *He's going to kill me now . . .!*

'Please, don't!' he cried. 'I don't want to die!'

Lymon grinned down at him. 'No one's gonna die, fatso. Not as long as you do what I say. Get up and get dressed.'

But Rose couldn't move. He was literally paralysed with fear. At the same time he was shaking so hard his large belly was quivering under the bed clothes like an immense mound of jelly. Beside him Beth stirred. Then she saw Lymon and the gun and gave a shriek of fear.

Lymon turned the gun on her. 'Shut up, you stupid

cow. One more sound from you and it'll be your last.'

Rose felt her fingers dig frantically into his arm. 'Harry!' she gasped. 'What's happening . . .?'

'I said shut your cake-hole!' snapped Lymon. She fell silent. The barrels of the shotgun swung back to Rose. 'Get up, fatso. Fast. We're movin'.'

'Where . . . where are you taking me?' he stammered.

'You're comin' on the job with me.'

'*Me*? But I never go on jobs! Never!'

'Well, you're comin' on this one. I figure it's time you got to see the other side of our business. You've had it cosy all these years sitting back behind your desk while other poor sods took all the risks.'

'But . . . but . . .'

'I said come on!'

Rose forced his body to obey his commands. He managed to sit up in bed. Then he said, 'Do you mind . . . waiting outside. I want a bit of privacy with Beth before we go. I have a few things I want to say to her . . .'

Lymon considered this then said, 'Okay, but be quick. I'll give you a minute. One minute. You're not outside dressed and ready to go, I'll drag you out.' Lymon nudged him in the belly with the muzzle of the gun. 'Understand?'

Rose nodded. Lymon then left. As soon as the door closed behind him Rose quickly got out of bed and stripped off his pyjamas.

'Harry, what's going on?' Beth asked him in a frightened voice. 'Why has he got a gun? Shall I call the police . . .?'

'*No*, you idiot!' he hissed at her. 'I'll explain everything later — if I get the chance.' He hurriedly pulled on his clothes then took the .38 from his dressing gown and slipped it into the pocket of his suit coat.

Then he left without another word to her.

'This would be a lovely spot for a picnic,' said Makepeace. 'If it was summer . . .' She took a sip from her cup of coffee that she was holding in both hands to warm them.

'It sure is a lovely place for an ambush,' said Dempsey. 'You got to give Lymon credit — he knows his stuff. Except this time he's gonna be the one who gets ambushed.'

The three S.I.10 vehicles were parked well away from the road so that they were completely concealed by trees. It would be at least an hour, according to the fat man, before Lymon would be arriving in his truck but everyone was staying out of sight of the road just to be safe.

Spikings, also holding a cup of coffee, approached Dempsey and Makepeace. 'How are you feeling?' he enquired suspiciously of Dempsey.

'Hey, all this sudden interest in my health is starting to bug me.'

'That doesn't answer my question,' growled Spikings.

'I feel fine. One hundred percent.' But in reality he wasn't feeling well at all. His neck ached, his head throbbed and he kept experiencing brief waves of dizziness but he was determined not to reveal his true state to the others. He looked about and took a deep breath. 'Ah, smell that English country air, huh? It's real good.' Then he paused and said, 'Is that a lark I hear?'

Makepeace smiled. 'Since when, Lieutenant, did you know the sound that a lark makes?'

'"Hail to thee blythe spirit!"' quoted Dempsey and, looking pleased with himself, added, 'Percy Shelley.'

Makepeace and Spikings exchanged a puzzled glance.

'See, you think I'm an ignorant New York cop.'

'Dempsey, how on earth did Shelley ever get to impinge upon your consciousness?' asked Makepeace.

'There was this English poet guy I used to know once — I met him in our drunk tank — and we used to hit his favourite bar together. He taught me.'

'He taught you Shelley?'

'Nah. He used to rub the neck of a bottle and make a sound just like a lark, or so he said. He loved doing that. Then he used to say, "Hail to thee blythe spirit, Percy . . ." Percy was the name of the bartender.' Dempsey looked up at the sky. 'Yeah, there was something up there that sounded like the neck of a bottle being rubbed.'

'Bloody hell,' muttered Spikings and walked off.

When he'd gone Dempsey took out a pack of chewing gum. He offered it to Makepeace. 'Better have some of this stuff, princess.'

She regarded it dubiously. 'Why?'

'Makes you invisible to the Bogeyman.'

'In that case I suppose I'd better.' She took a piece of gum and popped it in her mouth. Dempsey did likewise. 'Think he'll turn up today as well?'

'Who?'

'The Bogeyman, of course.'

He nodded. 'Could do. There's some kind of link between him and Lymon. I just wish I knew what it was.' He chewed his gum silently for a while, then said, 'I don't care what Spikings has told you. I don't want you sticking close to me. Lymon will probably be toting his favourite toy. A shotgun has a wide spread . . . you take care.'

'You too, Dempsey.'

Chapter FOURTEEN

Lymon told Rose to take the next turning on the left. They were driving through Stanmore in northwest London. Lymon sat in the back of the car with the shotgun resting on his knees. Rose had had no opportunity to use the .38 that was weighing down his right coat pocket, much to his relief.

The road was a cul-de-sac, ending with a pair of large wooden gates. 'Give three quick ones with your hooter,' ordered Lymon as they approached the gates. Rose did so and almost immediately the gates started to open. Rose saw a ferret-faced teenager with a punk hair-do and black leather jacket and pants.

'Drive through,' ordered Lymon.

Rose found himself in some kind of car junk yard. Several wrecked cars lay scattered about in various stages of decay and there were bits of engine parts all over the place, most of them rusting. In direct contrast to the general air of dissolution was a shiny red, obviously brand new Jaguar parked beside an old moving-van.

Lymon told Rose to get out. As he did so, he saw that the punk had already closed the gates and was eyeing him curiously. 'Who's that?' Rose asked Lymon.

'My driver.'

'Him? But he's just a kid!'

'He's not much younger than me. You think I'm just a kid?'

Rose didn't answer. The punk came over to them. 'This the Mister Big you was tellin' me about?' he asked sarcastically. 'Doesn't look much to me.'

'Ah, that's where you're wrong, Sid. Mister Rose here has had a very successful career. For years he's been getting other mugs to go out and do his dirty work for him. Very clever, he was. But today he's gonna get his hands dirty as well. Aren't you, Mister Rose?' Lymon gave him a contemptuous grin.

Rose said quietly, 'You're calling the shots, Nick. Whatever you say.'

'Yeah, whatever I say.' He looked at his watch. 'Time we was moving. Sid, you got everything straight?'

The punk nodded. 'No worries, Nick.'

'Remember, give the security van a good head start after it passes you. But when you hear the explosion put your foot down.'

Explosion? What explosion? thought Rose worriedly.

'Leave it to me, Nick,' said the punk.

Lymon motioned with the shotgun that Rose should climb in the cab of the moving-van. 'I can't drive one of those,' Rose protested.

'*I'm* driving. You get in the passenger side. But you

try any tricks and I'll gut shoot you. And with your gut I can't miss, can I?'

Rose climbed into the cab with difficulty, uncomfortably aware of the revolver in his pocket. He prayed that it wouldn't bang against the side of the van. He knew that Lymon would kill him instantly if he realized he was armed.

He finally made it into the cab and sat there panting from the exertion as Lymon got into the other side. 'I'm going to have to lose weight. Beth is right — I can't go on like this,' he told Lymon in a friendly tone, hoping to lessen the tension between them.

But Lymon's answer chilled his blood: 'You've left it too late, Harry . . .'

Throughout the drive to Greenfield Road Rose debated with himself as to whether or not to use the gun. Maybe he could just pull it out, point it at Lymon and order him to stop the van and let him out. But how would Lymon react? He might think that he wouldn't have the nerve to shoot and just ignore the gun. Or he would fire the shotgun that was resting across his lap, the barrels pointing at Rose . . .

And even if Rose could summon up the nerve to pull the trigger, would he be able to take control of the van before it hit another vehicle or went off the road . . .?

He was struggling with this dilemma when Lymon turned into Greenfield Road. At that point Rose decided to just wait and see what happened when the truck reached the ambush point. Dempsey and the other S.I.10 cops would be waiting there by now. Maybe they'd be able to overcome Lymon before he realized he'd been double-crossed . . .

Then, half a mile down the road, Rose got a nasty shock. Lymon slowed down then turned off the road and stopped the moving-van behind some trees. 'This isn't the spot! It's another half mile down the road!' Rose exclaimed.

'I know,' said Lymon calmly, and looked at his watch. 'But there's been a change of plans. I did a recce along this road yesterday and found this spot. Not as good as the one you picked, I admit, but it's a lot nearer the main road. If what you said about the automatic alarm in the security van is true I wanna be off this road fast, know what I mean?'

'But you can't just ... just alter everything at the last minute like this!' protested Rose. He could see his one chance of deliverance fading away. Dempsey and his men were going to be too far away to help him.

'Yeah, I can,' Lymon told him. 'I just did. Now you just sit there and shut up. I got to get things ready.'

Lymon opened his door and jumped down to the ground, taking both the shotgun and the van's keys with him. Rose next heard him opening the rear doors.

Rose sat there trying not to panic. The sweat began to pour off him, despite the cold, and he wound down his window. Desperately he wondered what to do next.

Then he remembered the .38 in his pocket.

He reached in and took hold of it. It felt reassuringly heavy. Solid. He took it slowly out, his mind made up. It was now or never ...

He aimed it towards the open driver's door, holding it with both of his pudgy, sweating hands. When Lymon raised his head into view as he climbed back into the cab, Rose would fire. He'd shoot the sod right between the eyes when he was at his most vulnerable.

Rose waited impatiently, his arms trembling. Now that he'd made up his mind he couldn't wait to get it over with. But he could still hear Lymon doing something in the rear of the vehicle . . .

Damn.

He could feel his heart pounding alarmingly. It would be funny if his heart gave out just as he shot Lymon, he told himself. Yeah, *very* funny . . .

Then it occured to him that he might not have the strength in his right forefinger to pull the trigger. The gun had not been used for years — its firing mechanism would no doubt be stiff after all this time.

So, using both thumbs, he pulled back the revolver's hammer. He'd been right — the mechanism was stiff. He needed all his strength to pull back the hammer until it clicked into position.

With the gun cocked he felt more confident. He was ready now . . .

It had gone silent in the back of the van. Lymon would be coming at any moment . . .

Dempsey looked at his watch again and frowned. 'Lymon's late. I don't like it.'

'Only ten minutes or so,' said Makepeace.

They and the rest of the team had taken cover in preparation for the arrival of Lymon's van but the deadline hour given to Dempsey by the fat man had come and gone.

Spikings, who was crouching uncomfortably nearby, his weapon drawn, said testily, 'I just hope your contact wasn't pulling a fast one on you, Lieutenant.'

'I'd bet my pension he was on the level. The guy was scared. You could smell it.'

'Yeah, but scared of *what?*' asked Spikings. 'Lymon or *you?*'

Come on you bastard! What's keeping you?! The tension was becoming unbearable for Rose as he sat there with the gun, now slippery with sweat, pointing at the open cab doorway. His ears were straining to pick up the sound of Lymon's approaching footsteps as he came back along the side of the van but all he could hear was his own pulse pounding in his ears.

Something cold and metallic touched him on the back of the neck. Then he heard Lymon's voice say, 'Gotcha.'

Rose wanted to scream. Lymon had somehow climbed silently up on *his* side of the cab. He shut his eyes, waiting for the shotgun to go off. He wondered what it would feel like . . .

'Raise the gun slowly,' ordered Lymon, 'And pass it back to me over your shoulder. But take your finger off the trigger first.'

Rose did as he was told. There were tears running down his cheeks now. 'How . . . how did . . .?' He couldn't finish the question.

'How did I know you were packing a shooter, you dumb lard bucket?' sneered Lymon. 'Because it was so obvious my granny would have spotted it. And she's blind.'

Rose felt the .38 plucked out of his trembling fingers. 'You're going to kill me now?'

'No. Not yet.'

Rose sagged with relief.

'Turn around and hold out your left hand.'

As Rose turned he heard a clink of metal then suddenly his wrist was encircled by the bracelet of a handcuff. The other cuff Lymon attached to a handle beside the door.

'I can't shoot you yet,' Lymon told him casually. 'Someone might hear the shot and come snooping around.' Then he jumped back down and came round to the driver's side. 'Plenty of time before the security van is due. Relax and enjoy yourself. Have a fag,' he told Rose as he climbed into the cab.

'You planned to do this to me all along, didn't you?'

'What do you think?'

'Why?'

'Come on, fatso. I know you grassed on me to that Yank copper. No one else knew I was stayin' at your place in Soho.'

Rose thought for a while then said, 'I've got a lot of money. In banks all over. Outside of England. Switzerland, Jersey ... You can have the lot. Every penny.'

'Yeah?'

'I swear it. Just let me live!'

Lymon shook his head. 'Thanks but no thanks. You see, I just don't trust you, fatso. I give you the time to get that money together and you'd probably pull a fast one on me.'

'No! No! I wouldn't! Please, Nicky, you've got to believe me!'

'Shut up and smoke your fag. It'll probably be your last one before you give up smoking permanently.'

Sid, sitting in the red Jaguar parked in the main road near the Greenfield turn-off, clocked the security van as it went by. He gave it two minutes then started the Jaguar's powerful, souped-up engine ...

'He's not coming,' said Spikings bitterly. 'It's almost time for the security truck to arrive. Your man has done us up like kippers.'

Dempsey didn't answer. He was thinking furiously. He knew that Lymon was unpredictable. Maybe he had changed the fat man's plans on the spur of the moment. Then he thought of the drive along Greenfield Road to this spot. There had been a couple of other places suitable for an ambush. Not as good as this one, true, but good enough at a pinch . . .

He made up his mind. He leapt up from his hiding place beside Makepeace and began to make for his Mercedes at a run.

'Hey!' yelled Spikings from behind him. 'Where the hell do you think you're going?'

Dempsey didn't answer. He had to do this on his own. If he was wrong yet again he didn't want Spikings and the others around as witnesses. And if he was right — well, maybe it was best if he took on Lymon alone. Less chance of anyone else getting hurt. Like Makepeace . . .

He reached his car, tore open the door and jumped in. On the way back to the road Spikings tried to block his way, forcing him to swerve and narrowly avoid hitting a tree, but he kept going, reached the road, made a screeching turn and then put his foot down.

Lymon ran back to the moving-van and swiftly climbed up into the cab, 'It's coming — and dead on time!' he said excitedly, more to himself than for Rose's benefit. For Rose the words were a death sentence.

Lymon started to count backwards, his eyes fixed on the wing mirror. He had left the van's motor running and now he was revving it up.

'Five . . . four . . . three . . . two . . . one . . . zero!'

The van lurched backwards, reversing until its bulk blocked the road. Lymon had timed it perfectly. The driver of the armoured van had no chance to avoid a collison. Even as he tried to apply his brakes the security van ploughed into the side of the bigger vehicle. There was a loud crunching of metal, a tinkle of broken glass and then silence.

While Rose sat dazed from the shock of the impact Lymon leapt down from the cab, carrying a canvas satchel. He ran round to the side of the security van, removed two stun grenades from the satchel, pulled their pins and rolled them under the van. Then he ran to the rear of the vehicle and attached a magnetic limpet mine to the door. He set the timer and backed away. At that moment the stun grenades went off with a noise that seemed to penetrate the ear drums like sharp, pointed sticks . . .

Lymon climbed back into the cab of the moving-van and pointed the shotgun at Rose. 'Thirty seconds before the mine goes off — enough time to take care of you, fatso.'

Rose closed his eyes and waited for the last sound he would ever hear.

Instead he heard Lymon mutter, 'Oh no . . .'

Rose opened his eyes. He saw that Lymon was staring over his shoulder. Rose turned and looked out the side window. He saw a grey Mercedes hurtling down the road towards them. 'It's that bloody Yank!' breathed Lymon in a mixture of surprise and anger.

Just then the limpet mine exploded, blowing out the back of the security van. The moving-van rocked violently from the force of the explosion, causing Lymon to almost lose his precarious grip on the side of the cab. Rose, seeing this, seized his opportunity . . .

He kicked out with his right leg, his foot catching

Lymon in the chest. Lymon fell backwards. As he fell he fired the shotgun but the blast missed Rose and perforated the roof of the cab instead.

As Lymon landed heavily on his back there came a simultaneous screeching from two sets of car brakes. Rose saw that Dempsey's Mercedes had come to a halt on one side of the moving-van while behind the armoured van Lymon's punk driver had arrived with the red Jaguar. He hunched down as far as he could, knowing that there was going to be a lot of shooting . . .

Dempsey cursed when he saw that there was no way he could drive around the van. He braked and jumped out, drawing his Colt Cobra as he did so. Crouching low, he ran round the rear of the moving-van. The first thing he saw was the wrecked security van with smoke pouring from its rear. Then, through the smoke, he saw Lymon running towards a red Jaguar, and trying to load his shotgun as he ran. Dempsey fired but the smoke spoiled his aim. *Hell*, thought Dempsey, *this is gonna be a repeat of the fiasco at the building site* . . .

Then he saw Lymon reach the Jaguar. Lymon turned, raising the shotgun. Dempsey ducked back round the corner of the moving-van as Lymon discharged both barrels. The deadly hail of pellets peppered the side of the van. Dempsey stepped out again . . .

Lymon was diving into the rear of the Jaguar which was already going into reverse. Dempsey got a glimpse of a startled young face behind the windshield before his next bullet hit it, causing it to go opaque.

But the Jaguar kept reversing at speed. Dempsey fired again, aiming at the engine . . .

The Jaguar was now about thirty yards away. Then it

backed sharply off the road, lurched forward in a tight turn and sped off.

Dempsey stood there firing at it until he knew it was out of range. Frustration raged through him. Lymon had got away *again*! His only hope was that one of his bullets had hit him, but with Lymon's luck that was unlikely . . .

Chapter FIFTEEN

Lymon peered anxiously through the rear mirror for any sign of pursuit even though he was confident that the moving-van had effectively blocked off the road. He was seething with anger. That bloody Yank had screwed him up again! He had been *that* close to getting his hands on all that money in the security van and up pops that Yank! And Rose! That fat bastard had set him up again too! The Yank must have been waiting at the other ambush point down the road . . .

'Nick . . .'

'Shut up and drive!' Lymon snarled.

'Nick . . . I been hit.'

'What?'

'When I was turning back there . . . bullet came through my door . . . I think I'm hit bad . . .'

'Damn!' Lymon leaned over the back of the driver's seat. He saw that there was blood oozing out of the punk's side. The bullet hole was about where his rib cage ended. Yeah, that's bad, thought Lymon bitterly. Aloud he said, 'It's nothing. Keep going until we reach the main road then I'll take over. We can't afford to get blocked off down here. Can you manage that?'

'Yeah . . . I think so.'

'Good on yer, kid,' said Lymon encouragingly.

'But Christ, Nick, it *hurts.*'

'Don't worry, there's a quack I know who'll patch you up in a jiffy. I'll take you straight to him.'

'Will you, Nick?'

''*Course* I will, mate,' Lymon lied.

As Dempsey helped the dazed and battered security men out of the wreckage of their vehicle he heard the sounds of brakes on the other side of the moving-van and he knew that Spikings and the others had arrived. He wasn't looking forward to seeing Spikings again . . .

Makepeace was the first to appear. She came round the front of the moving-van at a run, her .32 revolver in her hand.

'Relax princess, it's all over,' Dempsey told her. She looked around, taking in the wrecked security van and the three guards who were sitting on the roadside with stunned expressions on their faces. One of them had a bad nose bleed.

'Where is . . .?' she began.

'Got away. Again,' said Dempsey as Spikings, Chas and the others came charging into view, all their guns in their hands. Dempsey took a deep breath and faced Spikings. 'Lymon got away, Chief. In a red Jaguar. Number plate had been spattered with mud.

Driver was a kid. With a Mohawk hairdo.'

Spikings opened his mouth to say something to Dempsey but obviously changed his mind. Instead he turned to Chas and snapped, 'Get on the radio and send out an APB on that car! and call an ambulance for those men there!'

'Right, guv,' said Chas and ran off.

Dave Barnes, who had climbed up to check the driver's cab of the moving-van cried, 'Hey, there's someone in here!'

Dempsey pushed past Spikings and joined Barnes. He looked in the cab and saw, crouching on the floor with one wrist handcuffed to a handle, the fat man.

The fat man grinned apologetically and said, 'Do you think you could get me out of these cuffs? I have a rather pressing need to take a very long leak.'

About a half mile down the main road Lymon told the punk to stop the car. Sid did so gratefully. As Lymon got out of the rear door he started to shift himself, painfully, over to the passenger seat. But when Lymon threw open the driver's door he grabbed Sid by the arm and said, 'Not that way, *this* way!' And he roughly hauled Sid out of the car. Sid screamed as he hit the road.

'Sorry mate,' said Lymon as he leapt behind the wheel. 'But you've become a liability. A *bleedin'* liability.' Then he slammed the door and roared off, leaving Sid — writhing in the roadway.

'So you're our informant,' said Spikings sourly as he inspected the freed fat man. 'What's your name?'

'Remember our deal. Freedom from prosecution, right?'

'*If* you delivered Lymon to us. And I don't see him around. Do you?'

'But that's not my fault!' protested the fat man, mopping at his sweat-soaked face with a large, stained handkerchief.

'A deal is a deal,' said Spikings. 'We don't have Lymon but we do have you. You're nicked, sunny-jim.'

Dempsey intervened. 'Hey, chief, the guy's right. It's not his fault Lymon switched locations. Besides, if word gets out we don't treat our informers on the level our flow of info is gonna dry up.'

Spikings glowered at Dempsey, then he sighed and said, 'I suppose you're right.' He nodded at the worried-looking fat man. 'Okay, the deal stands. Now tell me your name.'

After a long hesitation the fat man said, 'Harry Rose.'

'Never heard of you,' said Spikings curtly. 'How many jobs have you been behind?'

Rose thought for a moment. 'About twenty two — twenty three, I'm not sure.'

Spikings looked incredulous. 'Twenty three! That's impossible! I'd have got wind of you long before this. Long before!'

Rose shrugged. 'I guess I've been lucky.'

'Either that or there's more to you than meets the eye! Twenty three jobs! Bloody hell!'

At that moment Chas came hurrying up. 'Guv, just got a report from one of the local patrol units. They found a young bloke on the main road not far from here. Fits Dempsey's description of Lymon's driver. *And* he's got a bullet in him.'

Spikings looked at Dempsey. 'Appears you hit *something* at least.'

Dempsey asked Chas: 'How is he?'

'They say his chances of pulling through are fifty-fifty.'

Unexpectedly, Rose said, 'I demand police protection.'

Spikings turned on him. 'You demand *what*, old son?'

'Police protection. Lymon's still free. He knows by now I set him up again. He'll be after revenge. He'll try and get me no matter what the risk. I know him! You've got to protect me from him!'

'That's not part of our deal,' Spikings told him coldly. 'You're on your own, sunshine. And if you've pulled off twenty three jobs without me ever getting a whiff of your BO — and I still find that difficult to believe — then you're smart enough to take care of Lymon.'

'Actually, Chief, he's got a good point,' interrupted Makepeace.

'What the hell do you mean?'

'I mean that he's probably right that Lymon will try to get to him. So if we stick by him the chances are Lymon will come right to us.'

'Hey, she's right!' agreed Dempsey.

Spikings stared at the pair of them for a time and then threw up his hands in disgust. 'Oh, go and do whatever you want! You do anyway!' he growled and strode off.

Dempsey grinned at her. 'You wanna know something?'

'What?'

'All this time since you been here and you haven't once asked me how I'm feeling.'

'That's true,' she nodded. 'So how are you feeling, Dempsey?'

'Like a bag of used cat-litter,' he finally admitted.

Dempsey and Makepeace accompanied Harry Rose back to his St John's Wood house. When they pulled up in front of it Rose said nervously, 'You go in first. Lymon might already be in there. He could have taken Beth hostage . . .'

'Beth?' Dempsey asked.

'The lady I live with.' He glanced at his watch. 'No, she's probably at her hairdressing salon now.'

'You're kidnapped at gunpoint in your bedroom this morning and your lady goes off to get her hair done?' asked Dempsey incredulously.

'No, no,' Rose shook his head. 'You don't understand. She *runs* a hairdressing salon. Wild horses wouldn't keep her away from it. She thinks her staff are on the fiddle if she's not there . . .' He reached into his pocket. 'Here are the keys.' Dempsey took them. 'Stay with him, princess, and keep your eyes peeled. For both Lymon *and* the Bogeyman.'

Dempsey got out of the Mercedes and walked up to Rose's front door. He rang the bell and waited awhile. When there was no response he used the two front door keys and went in.

The house was in silence. Warily he crept through the front hall and into the living room. Then he checked the other rooms on the ground floor, finishing up in the kitchen. All were empty. Dempsey returned to the hallway and climbed the stairs to the first floor. He didn't really think Lymon would have come straight back here but then Lymon *was* unpredictable. Better to be safe than sorry.

It was when Dempsey was checking the main bedroom that he heard a rustling sound. It seemed to come from a large wall closet. He drew the Colt Cobra and slowly approached the closet, remembering how Lymon had sprung out at him from the alcove in old man Kelly's place.

With his left hand he reached out for the door handle. But before his fingers could touch it the door suddenly flew open. He recoiled instinctively as a screeching figure brandishing a golf club came hurtling out of the closet. He used his right forearm to block the club as it came swishing down towards his head, at the same time lashing out with his left hand. His fist connected with a chin and the figure collapsed with a high-pitched wail.

Dempsey found himself standing over a plump blonde woman in a blue housecoat. She looked up at him and shrieked, 'Don't shoot me!' Then began to scream hysterically.

He was still trying, unsuccessfully, to calm her down when Makepeace burst into the room, closely followed by Rose. 'We heard screams,' said Makepeace, gun in hand. 'What happened?'

Before Dempsey could answer, Rose cried, 'Beth! What are you doing here?'

The woman stopped screaming and stared at Rose in astonishment. Then she jumped to her feet, ran over to him and threw herself into his arms. 'I thought you were dead!' she sobbed.

'Why aren't you at the salon?' he asked.

'How could I go to work after what happened? I was going out of my mind wondering what had happened to you after that awful gangster took you away this morning.'

Rose stroked her hair. 'There, there, darling.

Everything's all right now.'

She pulled back from him. 'All right?! How can you say that? When you come home with *another* gangster!' She pointed an accusing finger at Dempsey.

'He's no gangster, he's a policeman,' Rose told her.

'A policeman? Don't give me that! He punched me on the jaw.'

'Did you?' Rose asked Dempsey, looking shocked.

'She tried to brain me with a golf club,' explained Dempsey. 'I didn't know who she was.'

Beth was staring at him. 'Policeman my eye! He's an American! How can an American be a policeman? In England, I mean.'

'It's a question I'm constantly asking as well,' said Makepeace.

Beth looked at her then turned back to Rose. 'And who's *she*? Another one of your cheap floosies, I suppose. And don't think I don't know about them!'

'I beg your pardon!' exclaimed Makepeace as Dempsey laughed.

'Er, she's a policeman too,' said Rose awkwardly. 'I mean, a police*woman*.'

'And she's not cheap,' said Dempsey, grinning.

It was obvious that Beth didn't believe a word of what Rose was saying. 'And just what are they doing here?' she asked him.

'Uh, they're going to be protecting me, from that man Lymon. So they'll be staying here for the time being . . .'

This piece of information seemed to affect Beth worst of all. 'Oh no!' she cried. One unwanted house guest was bad enough, but *two* of them . . .!!'

Dempsey and Makepeace exchanged a glance. 'Nice to feel wanted,' murmured Makepeace.

'Look, I need to have a long talk with Beth. Explain everything to her. Do you mind leaving us alone?' appealed Rose.

'Sure,' said Dempsey. 'We'll be downstairs.'

'And we'll try not to break anything,' Makepeace assured Beth as they left.

Down in the living room Dempsey said, as he collapsed into an armchair, 'He's sure got his work cut out up there.'

'Yes. I don't envy him.' Makepeace picked up a phone and began punching out a number. 'I'll just call Chas and see if there have been any developments.'

'Well?' asked Dempsey impatiently, after she'd got through to Chas.

'They've found the red Jaguar,' she said as she put the phone down. 'Abandoned in Harrow. Has to be the same one because there was blood on the floor.'

'But no sign of Lymon, of course.'

'No. He's done his vanishing act again.'

'What about the guy I shot? The punk.'

'Chas said he'll live. Your bullet nicked his liver and there was a lot of internal bleeding but he's been operated on and the doctors say he's out of danger. Chas has sent someone to question him when he regains consciousness.'

'Betcha it won't do any good. He won't know anything useful about Lymon. Lymon won't have told him anything. The guy's a loner.'

'But what about his friend?'

'Friend?'

'The Bogeyman.'

Dempsey frowned and gently massaged the side of his neck. The bruise was still deep purple. 'I dunno, princess. Maybe there isn't a link between them. Maybe it was just a coincidence.'

'But if he wasn't working for Miller and he's not a crony of Lymon's, *who* is he then? and why is he after you?'

'That, princess, is the million dollar question.'

It was over an hour before Rose came downstairs with Beth. She was looking very subdued.

'Make some coffee for our guests, will you please, dear?' Rose asked her. She nodded vaguely and went off to the kitchen without a word of protest.

'Sort things out?' Dempsey asked him.

'More or less,' said Rose as he sat down and lit a cigarette.

'How did she react when you told her you were a crook?'

'She was relieved, actually.'

'*Relieved?*'

'All those times I had to go off on secret business, Beth thought I was seeing other women. So she's relieved to find out all her suspicions were groundless.'

'That's a woman for you,' said Dempsey and stared pointedly at Makepeace.

The afternoon passed uneventfully until just before 6 p.m. when the phone rang. After some hesitation Rose answered it. Dempsey and Makepeace saw the blood drain from his face. He put his hand over the receiver and whispered hoarsely at them, 'It's Lymon!'

Chapter SIXTEEN

'Talk to him!' ordered Dempsey. 'And see if you can *keep* him talking.' He turned to Makepeace. 'Quick, radio headquarters and see if they can get a fix on where he's calling from!'

As Makepeace dashed out to the car, Rose said awkwardly into the mouth-piece: 'I didn't expect to hear from you again, Nick.'

There was a harsh laugh at the other end of the line and then Lymon said, 'You mean you *hoped* you'd never hear from me again, fatso. Well, too bad. Your luck's out.'

'What do you want?'

'I want you to know I'm comin' to kill you. You double-crossed me again, you bastard.'

'No! No, I didn't Nicky, I swear it!'

'Yeah? Then what are you doing back home already? If you weren't pally with the filth they'd still be grilling you. Trying to figure out what you were doin' in that van.'

'They *did* question me, Nicky. For hours. But they couldn't pin anything on me so they let me go.'

'Don't give me that crap! I didn't come over with the last batch of bananas. You did me up *twice* and I'm gonna kill you for it.'

'No, Nick, you can't. I've got police ...' And despite Dempsey's warning shake of the head Rose continued, 'I've got police protection!'

Again came the harsh, sneering laughter. 'You think that's gonna stop me, fatso? You know me. I'll take care of the filth *then* I'll take care of you.'

Rose pulled out his stained handkerchief and mopped at the sweat of his face. Dempsey saw that his hand was shaking.

'Unless ...' said Lymon.

'Unless what?' asked Rose eagerly.

'Remember what you said to me this morning? That you got a lot of assets stashed away. How long would it take you to turn them into hard, untraceable cash?'

'Rose swallowed noisily. 'Oh, uh, I'm not sure. I'd need at least a few days.'

'You got 'em. How much will there be all together?'

Rose paused. Then, 'Oh, nearly a quarter of a million.'

'Yeah? Pull the other one, fatso. More like half a million by my figurin'. And it had better all be there or I'm gonna cancel the agreement.'

'It will be, Nicky. Where do I have to take it?'

'I'll let you know later.' And then the phone went dead.

Rose repeated Lymon's words to Dempsey. He was

just finishing when Makepeace returned, looking annoyed. 'No good,' she told them. 'Not enough time.'

'So what am I going to do?' Rose asked wearily.

'Play along with him. Next time he calls say you've got the money,' said Dempsey. 'But just draw enough out to bait the trap. Say a few thousand that we can use as the top layer over a case full of torn up newspapers. When he tells you where to take it we'll go along to meet him.'

Rose looked doubtful. 'I hoped I was finished with him. For good.'

'Don't worry, you soon will be,' Dempsey told him.

Makepeace said, 'If Lymon is going to hold off until Harry raises the cash there's no reason for us to stay here, is there?'

Dempsey considered this, then he said, 'I think we should hang around, just to be on the safe side. You know how unpredictable the guy is.'

'I was afraid you'd say that,' sighed Makepeace.

After a meal, cooked by Beth, of chilli con carne and rice the four of them sat in the living room watching television in a desultory fashion and not saying much, especially Beth. All of them were tired so it was no surprise when, at ten, Rose said, 'Beth and I are going to bed now. Will you two be comfortable down here?'

'Sure,' Dempsey told him. 'We'll take it in turns to take cat-naps on the sofa while the other one keeps watch. Now remember what I said about staying clear of the windows if the light's on in the room.'

'We will,' said Rose as he and Beth got up. They were just leaving the living room when Makepeace said, 'My God, what's that?'

They could all hear an approaching rumble.

'Sounds like a juggernaut lorry,' said Rose, puzzled. 'But we've never had one come along this road before . . .'

The noise got louder.

Dempsey suddenly remembered Lymon's ploy with the cement truck on the building site and how he'd driven it straight through the cabin. He leapt to his feet, drawing the Colt Cobra. 'Makepeace!' he yelled. 'Get them out the back door! Now!'

Makepeace didn't hesitate. She jumped up and herded the confused couple through the doorway.

Dempsey rushed to the front window and peered out. He was just in time to see two great blinding headlights as the huge truck flattened the small front fence. He paused to fire one shot through the window at the driver's cab before turning and running for the doorway.

Just as he reached the doorway the juggernaut came crashing through the wall of the living room in an explosion of glass, plaster and masonry.

Dempsey skidded into the hallway and made for the kitchen. Behind him the terrible sounds of destruction continued and he realized the truck was following him *through* the house . . .

Makepeace and the others were just disappearing out the back door as he entered the kitchen. 'Keep going!' he yelled. Then he glanced over his shoulder to see the kitchen wall bulge slowly inwards, then start to disintegrate. The sidebroad full of crockery in front of it exploded, sending fragments of cups, plates and saucers all over the kitchen. Then he saw the front of the truck appear . . .

He dived out through the back door. 'Keep going!'

he cried to the others. 'To the end of the garden! He's trying to drive straight through the house!'

When they reached the end of the garden they looked back towards the house. Dempsey expected to see the juggernaut emerge through the rear of the kitchen but though the truck's engine roared and the whole building shuddered and shook this didn't happen.

'I think he's stuck!' announced Dempsey over the din. 'I'm going back inside . . .'

'No, Dempsey!' cried Makepeace, but he ignored her. He ran back down the garden and stepped through the now buckled kitchen door. The kitchen was full of choking dust from the pulverized plaster and though the roar of the nearby engine was deafening Dempsey couldn't even see the front of the vehicle. Why is it, he pondered bitterly, that whenever I get close to Lymon's he's protected by a goddamn smoke-screen?

Then, abruptly, the sound of the engine ceased. Dempsey pressed himself against the wall, straining to see through the dust. Then he heard a crunch of glass. Dempsey lunged towards the sound. Almost immediately he collided with a body. He struck out with the heavy barrel of the Colt and was rewarded with a grunt of pain as it connected. But then he in turn received a crack across the side of the head with a hard object. A wave of dizziness overwhelmed him and for a few seconds he lost consciousness . . .

The next thing he knew he was sprawled on his back and Lymon was standing over him holding the shotgun. Lymon's face was twisted in a feral grin of triumph. 'Well, well, look what we got here. The Yank. Bye, bye, Yank . . .'

As Lymon's fingers began to tighten on the trigger

Dempsey shouted, 'Wait! Don't shoot or you'll kill yourself too!'

Lymon hesitated. 'Nice try, but it's too late for tricks. You're a second away from being raw meat.'

'The gas, Lymon! Can't you smell it? It's everywhere. You must have busted a gas pipe coming in here. You fire that shotgun and ka-boom!'

Lymon sniffed the air and realized Dempsey was telling the truth. He frowned, obviously wondering what to do next . . .

Dempsey turned his gaze past Lymon and said with a grin, ''Bout time you got here, Makepeace . . .'

As Lymon spun round Dempsey sprang forward and grabbed Lymon round the ankles, then gave them a savage jerk backwards . . .

Lymon fell faceforward with a bone-crushing crash. Dempsey was instantly on him. He pulled the shotgun from his grasp, sunk a knee hard into the small of his back, wrenched his right arm up behind his shoulder and then proceeded to bang Lymon's head against the floor until he stopped struggling.

'And I thought you were a pro,' sneered Dempsey. 'You're just a punk kid. A kid who fell for the oldest trick in the book.'

Lymon made a sound that was a cross between a snarl and a sob.

•

'Sorry about the house,' said Dempsey to Harry Rose. They were standing in the street watching as members of the Fire Brigade and Gas Board engineers warily entered the dangerously creaking remains of the Rose residence. The juggernaut lorry, whose rear protruded across the front garden, appeared to be the only thing still holding the house up.

Rose, his arm round Beth's shoulder, said shakily, 'Why? Why did he do it? I'd agreed to pay him. You heard me!'

'He never intended going through with the deal,' said Dempsey. 'His desire to get even had become stronger than his greed. The phone call was just a way of making sure you were home and putting you — and us — off-guard. And it almost worked . . .'

Makepeace came over and said to Dempsey, 'They're taking Lymon away. Want to say goodbye?'

'Yeah, Why not?' Dempsey strolled across to one of the several police cars parked in the street and peered in the rear window. Lymon, sitting handcuffed to a burly, uniformed cop, glared back at him. Lymon's nose was swollen and he had a black eye.

'See ya in court, Lymon,' Dempsey told him cheerfully.

'And I'll see *you* when I get out of prison, Yank. And it's gonna be sooner than you think!'

'Anytime, punk, anytime. But I just got one question for you . . . the guy with the rifle at the Miller job, and the same guy who was hanging around old man Kelly's place the night we had our run-in . . . he a pal of yours?'

The look of puzzlement on Lymon's face was enough to tell Dempsey all he needed to know. He slapped the roof of the car with the palm of his hand and the driver moved off.

Dempsey returned to Makepeace. 'I asked him about the Bogeyman. Didn't know what I was talking about.'

'He could have been lying.'

'No. I don't think so.'

'So where does that leave us?'

'Still in the dark, princess, still in the dark.' He yawned. I'm bushed. I'm gonna go home and hit the sack.'

'Me too. I've never felt so tired.'

'Wanna come back to my place, princess?' he asked, grinning at her. 'We could count sheep together.'

'Dempsey, the day they finally try and bury you you'll be chatting up all the female mourners at your funeral,' she told him wearily.

'You can't blame a man for trying, kid.'

'Oh, *yes* I can. See you tomorrow.'

Dempsey watched her walk off and gave a regretful sigh.

He could hardly keep his eyes open by the time he arrived at his flat. Once inside he pulled off his jacket and the shoulder holster containing the heavy Colt Cobra. He dropped both in a chair and dropped himself in another, conveniently close to a table on which stood a bottle of Jack Daniels and a bottle of Teachers whisky. He was just reaching for the latter when he heard a sound. Someone was in his bedroom . . .

He was back on his feet in an instant. Quickly he extracted the Colt from under his jacket and crept towards his bedroom door which was slightly ajar.

He kicked the door open and yelled, '*Freeze or I fire!*'

There came a very female yelp of alarm from the direction of the bed. It was Holly Headlong. She was sitting up in bed and staring at the Colt with wide, frightened eyes.

He sighed and lowered the gun. 'What the hell are you doing here?'

'It's my night off. I wanted to surprise you,' she said nervously.

'Well, you sure did that. And you'd have got a surprise too if I'd put a bullet hole through you. Never do that again.'

She got out of bed and slipped into one of his bath robes. 'Actually I've been here for hours,' she said as she came into the living room. 'I had planned to cook you a meal but as I wasn't sure when you'd be home I decided to wait. And a good thing I did . . .' She threw her arms around him and gave him a long, lingering kiss, then continued, 'When you didn't turn up I went to bed to wait for you and I guess I fell asleep. Aren't you pleased to see me?'

He grinned down at her and said, 'You know I am kid. It's just that I don't like surprises.' He guided her over to the armchair he'd been sitting in and collapsed back into it. Holly ended up sitting on his lap.

'But you gave me your key,' she pointed out. 'If every time I use it I'm going to be in danger of getting shot you can have it back.'

He reached around her for a whisky bottle and poured himself a large one. He said wearily, 'Keep it kid. Just give me a warning when you're coming. It's only a temporary situation. Soon as I collar that guy you saw in my hospital room I can relax again.'

'And when will that be?'

'That's a good question, kid,' and he took a large swallow of the whisky.

'Poor James,' she said and kissed him on the cheek. 'Are you hungry? Do you want me to fix you something to eat?'

He shook his head. 'No thanks. I'm too tired. Let's

just go to bed.'

'Fine with me.'

They got up, kissed again and were just heading for the bedroom when the phone rang. They both turned and looked at it.

'Don't answer it,' said Holly.

He sighed. 'I got to.' He went over and picked it up.

'Yeah?'

It was Makepeace. 'Dempsey, you've got to come round here right away! I think I've figured out who the Bogeyman is!'

Chapter SEVENTEEN

'You must be joking!' cried Holly in astonishment, as he put his holster and jacket back on.

'Afraid not, kid,' said Dempsey. 'I've got to go see Makepeace. She's got a hot lead on that guy I was telling you about.'

Holly folded her arms and frowned at him. 'Couldn't she have just told you this "hot lead" over the phone?'

'She said it's too complicated. She's got to talk it out with me in person.'

'Huh — I'll bet she does! It's probably just an excuse to get you over there. When you arrive you'll find the candles have been lit, the champagne's been chilled and the bed covers have been turned down.'

Dempsey couldn't help laughing at the idea. 'Boy, you sure don't know Harriet Makepeace.' He headed for the door. 'I'll be back as soon as I can.'

'Fine, but don't expect to find me here when you do.'

'Suit yourself, kid,' he said and left.

As the front door closed Holly muttered, 'Damn, damn, damn.' Then went back into the bedroom.

When Makepeace had put down the phone she turned and said resignedly, 'Satisfied?'

The man with the light blue eyes and the closely-cropped blond hair smiled and nodded. Then he gestured with the Browning automatic, fitted with a silencer, that she should return to her seat. She sat back down in the reclining, deeply upholstered armchair. He was sitting opposite her in a straight-back chair, the automatic resting on his knee. Her .32 was in his jacket pocket. 'You did very well,' he told her pleasantly.

'Dempsey won't fall for it. He'll be suspicious.'

'I don't think so. You were very convincing. You should have been an actress. And you would have had a longer life as an actress.' He gave her a benign smile that made her feel ill. 'Besides,' he continued, 'You're both very fatigued. Especially Dempsey. And fatigue makes you careless. Look how easily I was able to surprise you.'

She didn't need reminding of *that*. She was furious with herself. When she'd entered her living room and found herself face to face with this smiling, soft-spoken American she'd just stood frozen to the spot. He'd been able to disarm her without any difficulty at all. And she knew he was right about Dempsey. He *was* exhausted, as well as being unwell. The chances are he'd walk right into this trap. And there was nothing she could do about it.

She said to him coldly, ‘Who are you anyway? What’s this all about?’

‘What just about everything’s all about — business.’

‘And you’re in the business of killing people?’

‘You’ve hit the nail on the head, lady.’

‘And Demspey is your target?’

‘Right again.’

‘Who hired you to kill him?’

‘Some people back in the Big Apple. People who are still very unhappy about the operation he busted before he came over here. You must know about it. After all, it’s the reason he *is* over here. He made things so hot for himself in New York he had to leave. But the people who hired me — they got long, long memories. And long arms, too.’

‘I see,’ said Makepeace slowly. So he had been nothing to do with Miller or Lymon after all. She frowned and said, ‘But you’ve had opportunities to kill Dempsey before and yet you didn’t. Why?’

‘Orders. The people who hired me don’t want this to look like a hit. They don’t want Dempsey’s friends back there — and he still has a few — to know they were behind it. So I had to make it look as if he got knocked off in the line of duty in this country.’

She nodded. The pieces were beginning to fit together now. ‘But if you kill him here in my flat, how is that going to look like being in the line of duty?’

He smiled his smile again. Makepeace felt a cold sensation moving up her back, as if a spider with icy feet was walking up her spine.

‘I came up with a new approach,’ he said, sounding pleased with himself.

‘Which involves me?’

‘Which involves you.’

There was a lengthy silence then Makepeace said, 'May I go to the bathroom?'

'No chance.'

'Please. I really *need* to go to the bathroom.'

'Lady, you're not getting out of that chair until I say so. I *know* you. You're as resourceful as hell. I been keeping tabs on you and your partner for weeks now, watching you operate, listening to your conversations . . .'

'What?'

He smiled. 'Yeah. I put a bug in your office phone. Needed to so I could find out what cases Dempsey was working on and where'd he be.'

'Impossible!'

'On the level. It was as easy as pie. Walked into S.I.10 dressed as a British Telecom engineer. No one even looked at me. The bug I put in Dempsey's phone could pick up the whole office.' He shook his head. 'I tell you, lady, security in this country sucks. You'd think with the terrorism and all, the Brits would be more efficient.'

'Why don't you write a letter to *The Times*,' she suggested.

'I might just do that,' he said seriously.

They sat in silence after that. Makepeace desperately tried to come up with a plan of action but couldn't. There was no chance that she could get out of the chair and reach him before he had time to put several bullets in her. That was the reason he'd made her sit in the reclining chair.

Finally came the sound she'd been dreading. Her door buzzer.

'You know what to say,' he whispered as he raised the gun so that it was pointing at her forehead.

She was supposed to call out, *Come in, Dempsey,*

the door's open! but instead she yelled, 'Dempsey, go away! Run!'

But he came in anyway, charging through the doorway with his Colt Cobra in his hand.

He froze when he saw the blond-haired man pointing the silenced Browning at Makepeace.

'Drop your gun, Dempsey,' said the man casually.

Dempsey aimed the Colt at him. 'You first, buddy. It's stalemate.'

'Not stalemate, Dempsey. I'll count to five. You haven't dropped that Colt Cobra I'll give your pretty partner here a third eye. And I promise you it won't be as beautiful as her other two. You shoot me and I guarantee I'll still be able to pull the trigger as I die. Take the chance if you want to. One-Two-Three-Four ...'

There was a thud as the big revolver hit the carpet.

The man smiled. 'Good. Now put your hands behind your head and stand against the wall.'

As Dempsey did so the man went and picked up the Colt, never for a moment letting his aim waver. Makepeace said, 'Dempsey, meet the Bogeyman.'

The man raised an eyebrow. 'Bogeyman?'

'Our pet name for you.'

'Cute. I like it.'

'So what's your game?' Dempsey asked him harshly.

The man told him, repeating what he'd told Makepeace.

When he'd finished, Dempsey scowled, 'Okay, so you got me. Let Makepeace go. She's not part of your contract.'

The man smiled. 'This is free of charge. I owe her for putting a bullet through my side. Besides, she's a vital ingredient in my new plan.'

'Which is what?'

'You two are going to kill each other.'

'You're crazy,' Dempsey told him.

'Oh, I don't mean you'll *actually* kill each other. But it's going to look as if you did, and that's what counts.'

Makepeace laughed uneasily. 'No one will believe that for a minute.'

'Oh, I think they will. Like I said, I've been eavesdropping on you two for some time. I know you got this little routine. Dempsey kids about getting you in the sack and you tell him where to get off. Cute stuff. Your pals in the office lap it up. But I'm going to make it look like it was all for real. By the time I'm finished doing some artistic set dressing on Makepeace here it's going to appear that her oversexed partner finally cracked and went too far. Makepeace shoots Dempsey in self-defence and Dempsey blows Makepeace away as his final dying act. Cute, huh?'

After a silence Dempsey said in a hollow voice, 'The guys at headquarters aren't going to swallow it. No way.'

'Oh, they may not *want* to but what alternative will they have?' Then he took Makepeace's .32 out of his pocket and switched guns, holding the .32 on Dempsey in his gloved right hand and the Browning on Makepeace in his left. He stood up. 'Time to go to work. I've got an early morning flight to catch and there's such a lot to do. You first, Dempsey, for obvious reasons. Step away from the wall and come a few steps nearer to me. This has got to be at close range . . .'

As Dempsey stepped away from the wall he brought his right arm down in a blur of movement then dived to one side. There came the sharp *crack* of the .32 but the bullet hit the wall where Dempsey had been. Then both guns dropped from the man's hands. He was staring down at the hilt of the throwing knife that protruded from his chest. His expression, a mixture of surprise and disgust, was that of a fastidious diner who has just discovered a large food stain on his shirt front.

'Impossible . . .' he gasped then fell forward.

'Cute, huh?' said Dempsey as he got to his feet. He came and helped Makepeace out of the deep chair. She clung to him for a while, taking deep breaths and trying not to cry. Finally she said, 'That was close.'

'Yeah. Good thing I kept his throwing knife on me. On the way here I taped it to my wrist. Just as a precaution. I didn't really suspect anything was wrong but I had a hunch I might need it soon.'

'I'll never sneer at your hunches again, Dempsey.' She pulled away from him and began to dab at her eyes with a paper handkerchief.

He held out an open packet of chewing gum. 'Take one, princess. Makes the Bogeyman vanish. For good.'

PROSPECTS 1 – PARTNERS IN BRINE

John Raymond

PROSPECTS

Pincy and his mate Billy are a couple of very likely lads. On the dole, on the Isle of Dogs and on the make, they always have a few irons in the fire. No scheme is too daft or too dangerous, as long as it looks like a potential earner. And however bleak things get, their PROSPECTS always look rosy. But the best – and the worst – laid plans can go awry . . .

Futura Publications
Fiction/TV Tie-In
0 7088 2993 7

REMO – UNARMED AND DANGEROUS

Warren Murphy & Richard Sapir

IT WAS GOING TO TAKE A DEAD MAN TO SAVE THE COUNTRY

He was the toughest cop in Brooklyn. Until he woke up one morning to see his own name in the obit column – and a new face in the mirror. The face came with a new name, a new ID, and a new job.

Remo Williams was going to be the Eleventh Commandment: Thou shalt not get away with it. And Chiun, a slight little Korean, a Master, the sun source of all man's physical powers, was going to show him how . . .

REMO – UNARMED AND DANGEROUS

Futura Publications
Fiction/Film Tie-In
0 7088 3137 0

All Futura Books are available at your bookshop or newsagent, or can be ordered from the following address:
Futura Books, Cash Sales Department,
P.O. Box 11, Falmouth, Cornwall

Please send cheque or postal order (no currency), and allow 55p for postage and packing for the first book plus 22p for the second book and 14p for each additional book ordered up to a maximum charge of £1.75 in U.K.

Customers in Eire and B.F.P.O. please allow 55p for the first book, 22p for the second book plus 14p per copy for the next 7 books, thereafter 8p per book.

Overseas customers please allow £1.00 for postage and packing for the first book and 25p per copy for each additional book.